RACHEL SINCLAIR
INSANITY DEFENSE

By Rachel Sinclair

Southern California Legal Thrillers

Presumed Guilty
Justice Delayed
Insanity Defense
Wrongful Conviction
The Trial

Vinci Books

vinci-books.com

Published by Vinci Books Ltd in 2025

1

Copyright © Rachel Sinclair 2019

The author has asserted their moral right to be identified as the author of this work in accordance with the Copyright, Designs and Patents Act 1988. This work is a work of fiction. Names, characters, places and incidents are the product of the author's imagination or are used fictitiously. Any resemblance to actual persons, living or dead, places and incidents is entirely coincidental.

All rights reserved. No part of this publication may be copied, reproduced, distributed, stored in any retrieval system, or transmitted in any form or by any means, including photocopying, recording, or other electronic or mechanical methods, nor used as a source for any form of machine learning including AI datasets, without the prior written permission of the publisher.

The publisher and the author have made every effort to obtain permissions for any third party material used in this book and to comply with copyright law. Any queries in this respect should be brought to the attention of the publisher and any omissions will be corrected in future editions.

A CIP catalogue record for this book is available from the British Library.

Paperback ISBN: 9781036702922

Printed and bound in Great Britain by Clays Ltd, Elcograf S.p.A.

Chapter One

AIDAN

I WOKE up and looked at the person next to me. It was Regina. My head was splitting and I tried to desperately think about what had happened the night before. As I looked over at my nightstand, I saw a clue as to what might've happened. A joint was in the ashtray, which was pretty much par for the course for me on a Friday night. But next to the joint was an empty bottle of vodka. Grey Goose. I had pretty good taste when it came to vodka, just like my sister.

I nudged her. "Hey, you better wake up."

She turned over and looked at me, her green eyes squinting in the sunlight pouring in through the sliding glass door. She put her hand on her forehead and then put both of her hands on each side of her head, as if she was trying to steady it. She made smacking noises with her lips, as if she was trying to get something out of her mouth. Then she shook her head.

"What the hell happened? What am I doing here?" She looked down at her body, which was naked, and, I must say, beautiful. Then she looked at me. "Well, I guess that settles it. I guess you and I hit the sheets last night, although I have no idea how that happened. Maybe you can enlighten me."

There would be no enlightenment from me, unfortunately. It had been a long time since I drank to the point of blacking out, but, apparently, last night I broke that streak.

I wasn't too upset to be in bed with her. I had a crush on her from the very first time we locked eyes. But I knew she didn't feel the same about me. I knew she kind of thought of me as Avery's little brother and that was it. There was an age difference of eight years between the two of us, and I also knew she didn't date a whole lot. I knew why she never dated that much, as she had nothing but bad experiences with men over the years, so she really had no interest in getting involved with anybody.

Not that she was getting involved with me. I couldn't hope for that. The only thing I could hope for would be that maybe this could turn into an ongoing thing, a friends with benefits thing. That is if she was open to it. I had no idea if she was.

She covered herself up with a sheet and walked daintily to my attached bathroom. I looked down at her feet, as they strode across the hardwood floor, seeing how delicate they were. Her toes were painted a light pink and there were rings on just about every one of her perfect digits. On both of her ankles were tattoos. A rose with a saying on it was on her left ankle. It said *I'm not afraid, at least not to die. I'm afraid to live and not remember why.* On her right ankle was a picture of Winnie the Pooh and Christopher Robin, who was holding a balloon. I smiled, in spite of myself, seeing her tattoos. The Pooh tattoo was so unlike her, although the rose tattoo was totally her. That was her attitude - she was fearless. I would have to ask her a little later about the Pooh tattoo. Maybe it was meaningful for her, something she thought about from childhood.

I heard her rustling around in the bathroom, and I had the urge to join her in the shower. I pictured myself soaping her back, shampooing her hair, and banging her up against the wall.

I shook my head as I realized I had a woody just even thinking about it. What was I doing? What was she doing? Avery told me Regina had a policy to never shit where she sleeps, and that would, I would assume, include me. After all, Regina was Avery's right-hand woman and I was Avery's brother and roommate. Not to mention, Regina was over at our condo all the time.

I heard the shower running and I had to take my mind off my desire to join her in there, so I rolled a joint and walked over to my balcony. It was a Saturday morning, on Coronado Beach, which meant people were starting to pack the shores. There were people on the boardwalk, rollerskating, walking their dogs and gliding along on scooters and Segways. I took a deep breath, smelling the salt in the air, feeling the moisture on my skin, all while trying to keep my mind out of the gutter. It was no use, though. All I could think about was Regina's naked body and how beautiful it was.

Marijuana helped me think. It had the opposite effect on me than it did for most other people. I was not like my sister, who was typical of the people who smoked weed. She told me that all weed did for her was make her lay on the couch, delay responses to every question, and eat. A lot. She said that when she was high, if somebody asked her a question, she would answer it five minutes later. She didn't like the way that made her feel, so she rarely smoked with me.

But with me, it made everything a bit more clear. Everything burned a little brighter. It was like when you go to an eye doctor and you get glasses for the first time. The doctor would put you in that machine, where they ask you if this picture looks more clear or that one. And, at first, the picture would be extremely blurry. But, after the doctor put his special lens over it, that picture would come into sharp relief. Crisp. That's how it was with me with I smoked pot. Not that my world was blurry when I wasn't smoking weed, but it wasn't as clear as when I did. The clarity of mind was something that really was enhanced with every hit I took on the joint.

That was why I smoked as much as I did. I didn't do it for reasons other people would, to calm down or to feel the high. I did it because it cleared up my head and, at this point, knowing what I did with Regina the night before, my head needed some serious clearing.

I felt my stomach start to turn over and my head was starting to hurt. I was experiencing the first symptoms of a hangover - the first one I've had in a while, because I didn't usually drink to excess. I had gone through my days in college, and in law school, when I would binge drink with the best of them. A fun Friday night was having the guys over with a pony keg of beer, shooting the shit. They would crash on various couches, or on the floor, and the next day, we would have a hair of the dog that bit us.

But I was 26 years old now. I had a job. It was a decent job, with a law firm called Pierce and Wright. They were counting on me to not be a total fuck up. I was determined not to be.

At the moment, Pierce and Wright was giving me assignments where I appeared in court for various people who were involuntarily committed. There are procedures in California that protected them. A person who was a danger to herself and/or others could be involuntarily locked up for 72 hours without a hearing- a 5150 hold. This hold is for evaluation, and, if the person was no longer a danger to himself or others after 72 hours, that person was free to go. If that person was still a danger after 72 hours, they were subject to a 5250 hold and could be held for another 14 days, although they get a hearing, in the hospital, within 4 days. If the person was still a danger after 14 days, they're put into a conservatorship if the person's treating psychiatrist and the psychiatric medical director of the Public Guardian Office sign off on it. Called a 5350 hold, it actually refers to the fact that the conservator makes the decisions about whether or not the person stays in the hospital, not the patient.

One of my firm's specialties was involuntary commitment. I spent most of my time attending various 5150, 5250 and 5350 hearings. Often, the holds were justified, but sometimes, they weren't.

Just then, while Regina was still in the shower, and I was still staring out at the beach below me, my cell phone rang.

"Hey, Aidan, this is Stuart."

Stuart Williams was the managing partner of my firm and was responsible for giving me my various assignments. I was kind of surprised he would call me on a Saturday morning, but, then again, the law never sleeps and neither do our clients.

"Hey Stu, what's up?" I asked him.

"I hate to be bothering you on a Saturday morning. I really do. But one of our clients is in jail right now. Marina Vasiliev. She's been arrested for murdering her husband and she's been asking for you. She wants to hire our firm to represent her in the murder, but she's been very clear that the only person she wants to represent her is you. And she's also been very clear she wants you to come down and see her today. Probably within the next hour or two."

I shook my head, thinking about the splitting headache I had, and the way my stomach was turning somersaults. And I thought about Regina and how I really wanted to hang out with her that day. Not that she wanted to hang out with me. In fact, she probably didn't. But it was worth a shot to ask her.

And if there was one thing I didn't want to be doing on a Saturday morning, it was talking to Marina Vasiliev. She was one of the people I'd represented in 5150 and 5250 hearings. She'd been diagnosed with Borderline Personality Disorder and had been in and out of institutions for most of her adult life.

At the moment, at least before she apparently was arrested for killing her husband, she was back in La Jolla in the enormous house she shared with her husband, Lawrence Murphy. Lawrence was one of those new money guys who made a fortune founding a tech firm in Silicon Valley and leveraging it to found a series of biotech firms right here in San Diego. Biotech was the big industry in the area and was the main reason there was so much money flowing into the city. Everywhere I looked, there were condos going for a minimum of $1.5 million and houses that started at one million.

Lawrence was one of those rich guys. He was the CEO of a firm by the name of Pegasus, which was known not only for being on the cutting edge of discovering new pharmaceuticals, but also being on the cutting edge of human cloning. Animal cloning had been around for quite a while, ever since Dolly the sheep in the late 90s, but, as of yet, there has never been a human cloned. Pegasus was aiming to change that. It was not only involved with therapeutic cloning, which was relatively non-controversial, but was active in animal cloning and were stepping up their game in the race to make the first human clone.

As fascinating as I found Lawrence's job, I did not find Marina quite as fascinating, even though she was gorgeous. She had the kind of pale skin of somebody who never got out in the sun, which was very unusual here in sunny San Diego, and had hair the color of sunset. That was the best way to describe it, other than to say that I had seen her hair color on an Irish setter. It was a deep auburn, with streaks of blonde here and there. Her eyes were Cerulean blue, the color of one of the Blue Topaz rings I bought at a farmers market one day. She was delicate, as brittle as a bird, with slim shoulders, small breasts and a narrow waist. She was the kind of woman who, when she walked in the door, any door, most people turned to get a better look, not because she was odd, although she certainly was that, but because she was gorgeous.

But that didn't really matter. I still didn't want her as a client because she was certifiably off her rocker. She had the manipulative personality of somebody with a deeply rooted personality disorder, which she had. She would literally do anything to get people to do exactly what she wanted. Lying and digging up personal information to hold over people's heads were just a few of the ways she ensured everybody danced to her tune. Sympathy was another one of her calling cards. She would overdose on pills, slit her wrists, cry that somebody was raping her, even though it wasn't true. When all else failed, she resorted to violence. She would attack women and men, clawing their eyes out, kicking, scratching.

In short, Marina was a piece of work.

And, at the moment, she was a piece of work in jail. I

was fully prepared for anything she might say to me and I knew that almost anything she would say would be a flat-out lie. Nevertheless, I would try to get her story. She deserved to be represented by somebody and it sounded like that somebody would be me.

Just then, I turned around and saw Avery coming in the door. She was dressed in her jogging clothes, earbuds in her ears. She had her two dogs, Harlow and Lola, on a leash, and she was out of breath.

"Hey," she said. "What's going on?" she asked as she walked towards her bedroom. I wanted to tell her about what was going on and then I realized I did not want her to know Regina was still here.

"Not much," I said. "I have to see a client today. Which really sucks, because I was hoping I could join the guys later on in the surf." I was talking to Leo and the gang, buds of mine who I usually met with on Saturday mornings. We all made plans to get together about 1 o'clock. It looked like I wouldn't make that particular rendezvous unless I could cut this visit with Marina short, which was what I was hoping for.

I surreptitiously went into the bedroom and saw Regina was out of the shower now. She was dressed in the same clothes as she was last night - black T-shirt, torn and faded jeans, black boots. Her dark hair was up in a ponytail, and she had on no makeup. She still took my breath away, just as she always did. I was embarrassed to admit that.

What can I say, I'm a dude. Very visual and Regina was definitely pleasing on the eyes.

"About what happened here," I said to Regina. "Maybe we shouldn't tell Avery."

She just shrugged. "She's a grown-ass woman, she can

handle the fact that you and I hooked up last night. No need trying to hide it."

I had to admit, I kind of admired her *I don't give a crap* attitude, but I wasn't all that anxious for Avery to know I hooked up with her best friend and employee.

"Okay, if you insist," I finally said.

"I do insist. Unless you don't want me to let Avery know about us hooking up. And, by the way, this will be the only time. I'm sorry, dude, but sloppy seconds are just not my style."

Her words stung me just a little bit. I wasn't used to a girl treating me like a piece of meat. In fact, I was used to girls who got attached way too quickly. Obviously, that wasn't likely Regina's MO, and I had to admit that I kind of wished it was.

Regina went out into the living room, where Avery was standing next to a small table, sifting through mail. She glanced at Regina, and looked at the mail again, and then glanced up again. And then she cocked her head and smiled.

"I knew it was just a matter of time. What happened, the two of you got schnockered last night and did the deed?" she asked with a smile.

"Something like that," Regina said. "I think I had way too much Grey Goose last night. At least your brother has some taste, in vodka, I mean."

"Whatever, it's your guys' life. Anyhow, Aidan, what were you going to tell me?"

"I have a murder case."

Avery's eyes got wide. "You have a murder case? What do you mean?" She was clearly incredulous. Her mouth was opened and she was just staring at me as if I'd grown another head.

"Why do you say it like that?" I asked her.

"I mean, you've been a lawyer for like two seconds. You just got sworn in last month and your firm's already giving you a case like this?" She shook her head. "Dude, that's a malpractice case waiting to happen."

She was probably right about that. I hadn't been to too many court appearances as a lawyer, aside from a bunch of 5150 and 5250 hearings, which typically lasted not more than a couple of hours. I hadn't yet had a full-blown trial, with multiple witnesses, jury selection and an extensive discovery process.

I shrugged. "What can I say? She's one of my current clients. She was involuntarily committed to the psychiatric unit at Sharp, and she ended up in the Behavioral Health Center in La Mesa. She's been in and out of psychiatric units for most of her life and she landed in the hospital the latest time because she'd threatened to burn down her friend's guesthouse. The friend called the cops and Marina had a meltdown in front of the cops, threatening to kill herself, so she ended up in the psychiatric unit for a 5150 hold. She was deemed to be a danger to herself after the 72 hours, so she was held for another 14 days under a 5250 hold. I represented her in all of these hearings. And now, apparently, she's been accused of murdering her husband."

Avery looked at me. "So, you have a case now that might be capital, and you've been a lawyer for just a few months? What the hell is Pierce and Wright doing to you over there?"

"Sis, I don't know. All I know is that this woman apparently wants me to represent her in her murder case. And apparently she told my firm that it was me or nobody. And I guess she's got deep pockets because her husband was a billionaire. He owned this biotech firm called Pegasus, and —"

"You have the murder case of Lawrence Murphy?" Avery said. "Oh my God."

I took a deep breath. "That doesn't sound good. You immediately knew who I was talking about when I said what she did."

"Who doesn't in this town? Listen, Aidan, when a billionaire gets murdered, especially when the wife is accused of doing it, and especially when said wife has told everybody she knows that she didn't know if she did it because she'd blacked out the night of the murder, that's going to be a story. And here you are, a baby lawyer, hot and heavy in the middle of it. You're going to need some help."

"Well, I guess that's where you come in," I said. "And Regina. My firm doesn't have very good investigators for murder cases. I mean, our firm is a boutique firm, and it doesn't really like to stray from what they do, which is involuntary commitments and class-action lawsuits. I'm going to have to ask my direct supervisor if we can bring Regina on the case. I'm sure that won't be a problem. I'm going to need her help, because you're right, I'll be flying blind with this. The bad thing is, I really don't know why she wants me on her case so badly. I mean, to me, that seems kind of fishy."

"What do you know about this woman?"

"Just that she's borderline. That's her diagnosis. And, considering all the things she's done over her life, I think that's probably the right diagnosis. I mean, I can understand where her personality disorder came from. She was in an orphanage in Russia until she was seven years old. And God knows what happened to her in the orphanage. Her parents were murdered when she was three months old, and she spent all of her time from the age of three months to age seven in an orphanage.

I know a little bit about psychology. Actually, I know quite a bit about it, because that was my major in undergrad. She probably suffered from attachment disorder, which is what happens when a young child is neglected, abused or abandoned. She needed somebody to bond with when she was a baby, someone who could make her feel safe, and she never had that she was very young. I'd imagine she actually experienced horrors in that orphanage. I've read about them, about the kids who are beaten, starved, tied to benches and beds, and some are abandoned. I never really got into her orphanage experiences with her. I'm going to have to definitely talk to her psychiatrist, and her psychotherapist, and everybody who has been working with her to get the entire story about her."

"Okay, so she's borderline. Does she have any lapses of time?"

"I think she does. At least, that's what she tells me. She does tell me, or she has told me, that she would lose entire days sometime. Like it would be Friday afternoon, and the last thing she would remember would be going to the movies the previous Monday. She would have no clue about what happened between those two periods of time. So, yeah. She definitely has had lost time. They call it dissociation."

"So then it's possible that she killed her husband and just doesn't have any memory of it." Avery said. "You're going to have to find out what happened to her."

I looked over at Regina, who was nodding. "Aidan, I'll come with you down to the jail. You want me on this case, right?"

"Of course, you're the best." I clasped my hands in front of me, suddenly feeling shy. This was Regina, a girl I'd known for years. I wasn't used to this. I wasn't used to having my one-night-stand around me after the night had passed. I could smell the scent of her slightly woodsy perfume, could taste the strawberries that were on her lips the night before. I took a deep breath, trying to keep myself from having a boner. That would be embarrassing, to say the very least.

Was my working relationship with Regina going to work? Now that we had broken the seal, so to speak, were we going to be able to just go back to the way we were? This was uncharted territory for me. I wasn't used to seeing my one-nighters again. I was used to women who knew the score, just like I did. Just one night, boom boom boom, and that's it. Yet here I was with my one-nighter going with me to the jail to see his Marina person.

What had I gotten myself into?

"Marina's waiting for us?" Regina asked me.

"She is. Of course, were is she going to go?"

"True that. You driving?" Regina asked me.

"Yeah. I'll buy you lunch."

"You don't have to do that. I got stuff I gotta do in the afternoon."

We said goodbye to Avery, got in my car, and headed towards the jail.

Chapter Two

REGINA and I went to the San Diego County jail and waited for Marina to be brought out. I looked over at Regina, who had her hands clasped in front of her, not saying a word. I wondered if she was thinking the same thing I was, which was that last night was a mistake, although it was definitely a mistake I'd like to keep repeating. Not that I could say that to her.

"I was looking at this case, on my phone, on the way over here. What's with this Pegasus thing? They're trying to do human cloning over there?" She shook her head. "I mean, why? That's so weird. Do you remember, God, it was about 20 years ago or more, there was some weird couple on some island who said they'd cloned a human ? And did you ever read that book, *The Boys from Brazil?*"

"No, I can't say I've read that book," I said, impressed that Regina had. I'd heard of that book, but I didn't really know what it was about.

"Well, in this book, these mad scientists cloned Hitler, over and over again, all these new Hitlers, I forget exactly how they were able to do it, because you know Hitler has been dead for so long, but they cloned him. And then they would take these boys, these Hitler clones, and kill their fathers at a certain time, things like that. Because they wanted the baby Hitlers to have the same experiences that Hitler went through. You know the whole nature versus nurture thing. Was Hitler born bad, or was he made that way? Anyhow, these crazy guys wanted these kids to have the same experiences that Hitler did, so they made sure these kids' fathers died at the age of thirteen, or whatever, and they made sure that the father was married to a much younger woman, because those were Hitler's life experiences and the new Hitlers had to have the same experience. I don't remember exactly how it ended. I really don't know what the point is in human cloning. What purpose does it serve?"

"Well, maybe some rich person is going to want to have his daughter cloned because who knows why. I agree with you, however, I do know that cloning has been extremely beneficial in the medical field. You can –"

"I know. People could clone themselves so that they can have excess body parts. You know, you create somebody, exactly like you, and you could store your clone in some laboratory somewhere and just take their liver, or whatever, if you need it. I think I saw a movie like that too, with Scarlett Johansson and Ewan McGregor. I mean, why else would cloning even be a thing?"

"I admit, I don't know. Probably Pegasus just wants to be the first. Just like putting a man on the moon - what was the point in that? I don't really know, but it was important to be the first. Human cloning will be like that."

Regina rolled her eyes. "Yeah, maybe it was pointless to put a man on the moon, but, at the rate we're going, we might have to put people up there to live once we destroy this planet. Besides, the space program has brought a lot of great things to the world, like satellites." She shrugged. "I don't know, but I agree the money going to the moon would probably have been better spent taking care of the people on earth."

Just then, Marina showed up. She was dressed in an orange jumpsuit, of course. Her hair was pulled up in a ponytail and she was wearing no makeup. Still, even though she was extremely pale, she looked like a supermodel. Her blue eyes were clearer than ever, and she walked with the grace of a leopard. Her full lips were pursed as she looked at Regina and me. She was not in handcuffs, either her wrists or her legs, because this was a professional visit, so it wasn't necessary to shackle her.

She sat down at our table, and then looked at Regina and me with suspicion in her eyes.

"Aidan," she said, looking at Regina. "Who is this?" Her eyes bored holes in me. "Aidan, are you cheating on me?"

She smiled as she looked over at Regina and put her hand on Regina's arm. "Soft. You must use good moisturizer. Because I can tell you've been in the sun a lot. You're very tan. You have the kind of skin I've always wanted for myself. Dark."

I was still trying to figure out why she asked if I was cheating on her. I was pretty sure this was meant to be a joke, but, who knows? It was entirely possible she had created a relationship between the two of us in her mind.

Regina just looked at me and shook her head.

Marina looked at me again. "Aidan, are you going to answer my earlier question? Who is this?"

"This is Regina. She's going to be my investigator."

"Investigator. Is that what they're calling it these days?"

She looked at the two of us and smiled. "I can smell it on the two of you. Pheromones. I have a very keen sense of smell. You guys are doing it." She leaned back. "Not that I care. You can do what you want, of course. I just don't know if your lover should be working for you. You're going to get distracted and you're going to do a poor job on my case. That's all I'm thinking."

I didn't try to set her straight. How could I? She somehow picked up on the nonverbal cues between Regina and I, and she had both of our numbers.

"Trust me, Regina is nothing but a professional. And a great private investigator."

"I'll bet," she said.

"And I'm a professional. I won't get distracted by Regina."

"You're a professional?" Marina said with a snort. "You're just a baby. A kid. You're the legal equivalent of Doogie Howser."

"Yet you want me on the case, right?"

"Yes, I do. You see, you're eye candy, Aidan. If I have to go through a nightmare such as a murder trial, when, if you ask me, I should be getting a medal for that man being dead, I might as well go with somebody who's sexy. Like you."

"Marina, that is not the way to pick an attorney," I said, stating the brutally obvious.

"You think I care? Listen, I really don't care whether I live or die. I don't care if I go to prison. I don't care if they put a needle in my arm. I think it would be kind of electric. Just think about all those people on the other side of the glass, watching me die. It gives me shivers of excitement just thinking about it. Also, just think about all those people I can meet behind bars. All the trouble I can stir up.

Quite frankly, I'm very bored with my life as it is. Why do you think I go into the hospital all the time? I live for different experiences, and there's nothing more thrilling than being in a place where people are constantly brought in screaming. Prison is a place where all these damaged lost souls are. All the scared people, all the people who've been tortured throughout their lives. What can I say, I like twisting the knife a little harder. Especially if you're weak. If I go to prison, I'll have my pick of people I can torment."

Regina stepped on my foot, but I was still watching Marina. Regina put her pen down, as she had stopped writing and was just watching Marina with me.

It was then that Maria smiled. "I gotcha, didn't I? You thought that's really what I was after, didn't you? You thought I really wanted to just go to prison so I can torment weak people." She shook her head. "No, that's really not it. I want you to be my attorney, because, quite frankly, I trust you. When you went to my hearing for me, I thought you did a good job. My husband is a billionaire, and believe it or not, I was able to take control of my own personal bank account, don't ask me how I got the money, because you know my husband's assets are frozen at the moment. So I can't get into it. I have my own money, not much, just about $8 million in there. So I can pay you what the firm is asking. One thousand dollars an hour. I just want to have an attorney I like. It's nothing more than that. Besides, six of one, half dozen of the other. Attorneys are all the same. I'm sure you'll do a good job."

Regina resumed her note taking.

I just watched her some more. I didn't know which statement to believe from her - that she wanted to go to prison for sadistic reasons or that she was joking about it.

I decided just to stop trying to figure out the answer to that question, because it was making my head hurt.

"Okay, Marina, I need to ask you some questions about the night your husband died."

She leaned back in her chair. "Go ahead. By the way, you have to get me out of this place. This place stinks like you wouldn't believe, and, quite frankly, this color clashes with my skin and hair. Redheads look horrible in most oranges, especially this particular shade. And the food, don't even get me started. Inedible is not the word."

"I'll do what I can to get you a bond you can make."

"Good," she said. "I have about $5 million to spend on my bond. The rest of my money I have to use to pay for you sharks."

"I'll bring it up at your arraignment," I said. "Now, tell me about the relationship you had with Lawrence."

Marina snorted, which was an odd sound coming from such a small dainty woman. She pursed her lips and I looked away.

"What's there to tell?" she finally said. "I married him for money. Of course. He married me because of the way I look. There wasn't any sex between us, so he wasn't getting much from me. And I certainly wasn't getting anything from him either. But, you know, he helped me to look right at his fancy parties. How not to make a total idiot out of myself in front of people. I needed to go to social functions with him and not drool in front of people and pee on their floor. That's what I did. He had like this entire resumé for me."

"A resumé? What do you mean?"

"A resumé," she repeated. "When he married me, he gave me something that had my name on it and had a job description on there. It was so weird, really. He told me what was expected from me and that he would give me $1 million for every year we were married and no more. So, it kind of was like a job where I earned $1 million a year for not doing a whole lot."

That sounded weird, to say the very least. "I guess I don't really understand. Why would he hire you to be his wife, as opposed to finding somebody who would be his wife for real? The guy was loaded. I'm sure there are quite a few women who are more than willing to marry him."

Marina just shrugged her shoulders. "How am I supposed to know? Besides, the guy was gay. Well, maybe not gay, but definitely bisexual. I don't know the answer to your question, but you have to admit he got off cheap. I'm only getting a million a year, when the guy was worth billions. Any other woman wouldn't put up with that crap. You should be asking me why I got married to him, not the other way around."

"And if he died?"

"If he died, I get nothing more. My prenup says I only get a million a year, and if he died, all of his property goes to charity." She shook her head. "Charity. Not me. Makes me sick, but what can you do? At least you know I didn't kill him to get his money, because I'm not going to get a dime out of his fortune. All I got is the $8 million I've earned over these past 8 years, and I have to pay most of that to you guys. I'll be in the poor house in no time."

That was an interesting twist. It certainly would blunt the inevitable argument that she killed her husband for his money.

"Besides," Marina said. "Even though he was worth billions, most of his money was in Pegasus. I'd rather just take the cash. God knows I wouldn't want to take over for what he was doing there. I think it's unnatural, that human cloning nonsense. Where I come from, you don't do stuff like that."

"So I take it you were not approving of what he was doing?"

"Of course I wasn't. His company is trying to clone somebody just because they can. No other reason. But if they can do it, watch out. We'll have rich guys all over the world creating a clone just so they can have somebody to take over their money when they die, and maybe give them a body part or two along the way. And I read up on the process, with animals. There's always a genetic problem with the second animal, the cloned one. It's always sick. It always dies young. I think the sickest thing in the world."

"You do know that, even though your husband's dead, that cloning project will go on," I asked her. I was starting to suspect that maybe she killed him to stop the cloning project.

"Of course I know that. They got this weird scientist over there heading it up. Dr. Redmond." She shook her head. "You're just trying to nail me on this, any way you can. You're thinking I'm going to confess to killing him to stop him from cloning. I'm telling you I didn't do it. Or at least I don't think I did it."

"About that," I said, "you say you don't think you did it. But you told the cops you have no memories from the night he died. So how do you know if you did it or not?"

She shrugged. "I don't know. I don't remember that day. I don't remember several days before that day."

"So you really don't know if you killed him or not, right?" I asked her.

"I guess I don't." Then she smiled at me. "I guess I don't."

I sighed. "Listen, I'm going to have you evaluated by a

psychiatrist. I think we're going to have to think about trying for an insanity defense."

"You won't do that. I won't let you do it. I'm not insane," she said.

"Yes, I understand you think that," I said to her. "However, if in fact you killed him, and you were not aware what you were doing, which was entirely possible because you don't know what happened that night, an insanity defense would be the way to go. Listen, people kill people all the time and not remember what they did afterwards. If you had no idea you were murdering your husband, or if you didn't know at that time that killing was wrong, we can get you off with an insanity defense. An insanity defense is one hell of a lot better than trying to convince the jury that you didn't do it when you don't know yourself if you did or not."

She studied me for several minutes, not saying a word. She put one delicate hand up her cheek, and just looked at Regina and me. "No," she finally said. Then she looked away from both of us.

"No, what?"

"No, I'm not going along with that. I wasn't crazy that night, I just..."

"You just, what?"

"I just have times of my life when I don't remember what happened. That doesn't make me crazy. I know I've been in and out of mental institutions for most of my life. But I was never crazy. I've always known what I was doing when I was doing it."

I rolled my eyes. "Listen, if you have times in your life when you don't remember what you did, then, I hate to say it, but during those periods of time, you definitely weren't sane. Call them psychotic fugues, call them dissociative episodes, whatever you will, but you cannot say your brain is rational during these periods of time. You quite possibly could've killed a man while you were in this dissociative state, so, as I said, I want to plead you not guilty by reason of insanity. You'll be evaluated by a doctor and —"

At that, she stood up. She came after me, her eyes filled with unbridled rage. Even though I'm 6'2" and she was only 5'6" and extremely small, the rage made her stronger than 10 people. She got body blows on me before I even knew what was happening and she kicked me. She jabbed her finger in my eye, and pain shot through my skull when she did that. She screamed so loud that it sounded otherworldly. It wasn't quite the sound of a wounded animal - it was more high-pitched than that, and more desperate.

I couldn't react, because the rage came on so suddenly, seemingly out of nowhere. "I said I'm not going to go along with it and I'm not going along with it!" she screamed.

A guard came out and put the tase on her immediately. At first, it seemed she wasn't even affected by the the taser. As small as she was, the first tase didn't faze her. She just kept hitting and kicking me.

The guard tased her two more times and she finally crumpled on the ground.

"I'm sorry about that, counselor," the burly guard said to me. "She's been doing that a lot."

When I got my thoughts together, I realized I'd seen a side of her that was just a little bit spooky to me. The woman obviously had a lot of rage. She attacked a lot of people, both in the mental institutions, and, according to the guard, she apparently was attacking people here in jail.

She was definitely capable of violence. Did she kill her husband? Perhaps there was a clue in the way she described her relationship with her husband. She said they basically didn't have a real marriage and she was essentially being paid to be his wife.

Plus, I knew something about her background, about her stay at the orphanage when she was a little girl. I knew her mental illness came from very deep roots. She didn't know what had happened that night - an insanity plea would be the best thing for her. She would be evaluated by a psychiatrist, and if she ever recovered, she would be out.

I just didn't think we could win without an insanity plea. Even though Marina didn't really know if she killed her husband or not, the jury would have to trust me when I told them she didn't.

To win this case, assuming I couldn't go with an insanity plea, I would have to find another person who might have really done it. This wouldn't be the easiest thing to do.

The guard took Marina away and I looked at Regina, who was shaking her head and laughing. "Man, that chick's got some issues. To say the very least. You okay?"

"Yeah, she sucker punched me. I wasn't ready for her to turn into a wild banshee. I guess I probably should have been, considering this is what she does. Listen, I don't know how much investigation you're going to have to do in this case. I think it's just a matter of me having her evaluated by a shrink who can testify she wasn't sane at the time of the murder. I don't know if classic investigation will be warranted here. In other words, I don't know if you necessarily have to be looking for another culprit. I'm pretty sure she's the one who did this."

Regina looked annoyed, like her time was being wasted. Which it was. "Suit yourself. But, if you ask me, there are places you can really look to see who else might have had it in for this guy. I mean, think about what he does. He's the CEO of a company that's experimenting with human cloning. That's something that pisses a lot of people off."

I wanted to tell Regina the truth - I wasn't relishing trying this case. I wanted it to go away, and the best way that I could imagine it going away would be if I could have my client declared insane. Preferably not fit to stand trial. But, even if she was declared fit to stand trial, asking the jury to find her not guilty by reason of insanity would be the easiest way to win the case. I really didn't want to go the entire route of putting on witness after witness, trying to break them down and admit they had a motive to kill Lawrence, so the jury could believe a SODDI defense - some other dude did it.

I wanted to take the easy way out, in other words.

Yet I didn't want Regina to see me as somebody who would back down from a challenge. "I still think I'm going to have her evaluated for what she possibly knows about what happened that night."

"Dude, she told you she doesn't know what happened that night. You owe it to her to try to do at least some investigation to see who might've killed him. What happens if you try to go for not guilty by reason of insanity and the jury doesn't buy it? They might not. And then what? You'll be standing there with your dick in your hand. Not to mention a malpractice suit."

I opened my mouth and closed it. "Listen, you heard her. You heard what she was saying. She said she didn't care if she lived or died. Maybe that's right. Maybe that's the reason why she wanted to hire me in the first place. If she really wanted to win this case, she would hire somebody who's, you know, competent."

Regina shook her head. "I can't believe I'm hearing this. You're Avery's brother. Avery would never allow a client to push her around like that. Come on man, grow a pair. You're getting paid good money for this case, or your firm is. Do some investigation."

"Here's the thing. If I try to go with a SODDI defense, some other dude did it, I don't think I can also try to plead in the alternative that she was crazy and did it herself. So I have to go with one or the other. Personally, I think the insanity defense is probably the more likely scenario. It's more likely to win."

"We don't have to commit to an insanity defense yet, right? She hasn't even been arraigned yet. When do you have to put in that plea?"

I was embarrassed that I didn't know the answer to that question. I would have to do research on that, as I would on everything else in this case. I was in over my head, but, at the same time, I would have to do what I could to give this woman a good defense. "I don't know the answer to that question. I'm going to have to look it up."

"Figure it out. In the meantime, you have to figure out when you need to make that insanity plea, and, before that time comes, you can get some investigation done. I agree you probably can't argue in the alternative, at least to the jury. That doesn't make any damn sense. So you're going to have to go with one or the other, either SODDI or insanity. You know what direction I'm leaning, so I won't say any more."

We got up from the table and walked out to my car. "Okay. It's a beautiful afternoon. And I don't know about you, but I'm really anxious to get some surfing done. Would you like to come along?" I felt a little bit shy asking her, like I was asking her on a date or something. And, truth be told, that was exactly what I would try to do. I knew she surfed. She was pretty good at it. My plan was to get her out in the ocean with me, and then maybe little bit later, we would go to a bar and grab a drink or three. A couple of margaritas, chips and salsa, a good Baja burrito, and, with any luck, we'd have a repeat performance of last night.

Of course, she shot me down. "Sorry, Aidan. I got things to do. But you're going to have to think about this case. Give it some real thought. Find out who she knows, talk to some of the other patients at her hospital. Talk to some of her therapists, some of the coworkers of her husband, that sort of thing. I'll do any kind investigation you want me to, of course. Just let me know."

We drove along in silence after that. I was feeling a bit rejected. I didn't know what she was up to that day, but whatever it was, I knew it was not to be with me. And that kind of stung.

I got back to my condo and Regina headed over to her own car, which was parked on the street next to the condo. The weather was warming up, and there were already a lot of people heading down to the beach. I would be one of those people in just a matter of hours. Regina, however, was not going to be. And this pissed me off more than anything.

"Well, dude, later," she said. "You got my number, call me when you want to have some investigation done on this chick. Because I know that if you don't do it, you're going to regret it. Don't take the easy way out."

I walked away from her and said nothing. I was steaming, truth be told. And I didn't want her to know that.

Chapter Three

AS SOON AS I got into the condo, I got into my wetsuit. I grabbed my surfboard, which was out on the balcony, and headed out the door.

The sand was hot underneath my feet and I could see there were probably 20 surfers in the area where I would be. Some of my best bros were out there, paddling and waiting for a good wave.

Coronado was not always the best place to surf. In the San Diego area, Ocean Beach probably took that honor, since Ocean Beach typically had the biggest waves, as well as the most violent undertow. Coronado was relatively shallow, which meant the waves were not as big. But I didn't want to bother with putting my surfboard on the roof of my car and driving out to Ocean beach, which was about 20 minutes away without traffic. So I decided just to go ahead and take whatever waves I could get.

The wind was blowing just enough that the waves were halfway decent. I said hello to some of my buddies and they waved at me. One of the guys who was out here was

George Cooper, who was also an associate at the firm, although he had been around our firm a lot longer than me. I made a mental note to pick his brain about the Marina situation after we got done with our surfing.

I was out there for three hours, paddling, and then catching a wave and riding several all the way in. I was one of the better surfers out there because I'd been doing it for so long. Unlike Avery, I had grown up around a beach all my life. Our dad split from our mom when I was only two years old, and we ended up living in San Ysidro, a border town about a half hour away from our condo.

So a coastal town was the only thing I'd ever known. I'd been surfing since the age of four. I was one of those little kids on the beach with a blue and yellow wetsuit, listening intently to an instructor telling us how to paddle our tiny surfboards, and how to stand up on them, and how to ride them in. Surfing lessons was one of the few things my dad could afford. He never worked that much, pretty much going from one odd job to another.

After our surfing was over, George and I headed over to a seafood restaurant that looked out onto the water. We sat outside and drank margaritas, and I was wishing he was Regina. But he wasn't. He was somebody whose brain I could pick, however.

"So I guess you're in a dilemma, aren't you?" he said after I told him the story about Marina. "Listen, I know it's probably tempting to take the easy way out and say that the woman killed her husband in a psychotic fugue or a dissociative state. But I think your assistant, I mean your investigator, probably has a point. You don't know that she did it and neither does she. How does that even work?"

"I guess you make a point. If we're going to try to convince the jury that she's not guilty by reason of insanity, then she's going have to stand up and say she did it. Or we're going to have to ascertain she did it."

"Right," George said. "And you can't do that, can you? So what you're going to be doing is going to a jury and basically say you don't know if she did it or not, but if she did, she wasn't sane when she did. I don't know, I don't think that's all that persuasive."

I nodded and took a sip of my margarita. My California burrito, which is basically a regular burrito with french fries inside, arrived, and I bit into it. The cheese oozed out and I grabbed one of the fries and popped it into my mouth. It was the kind of greasy comfort food that made me halfway forget my dilemma at the moment.

"I guess you're right," I said. "Listen, I need to talk to James. Stu says he's the one who wants me on this case. I'm going to ask him if he wants to give me a second chair on this. Do you think you would be available for that?"

"I guess so. I mean, like you, I don't really have much experience with murder trials but I can try to muddle along. I know that doesn't give you much confidence, but what does this woman expect? Did she explain to you why she wanted you to be her attorney? She obviously could afford somebody who's, well, not a bad trial attorney. You don't know what you're doing. I know your sister knows what she's doing, but she's not the one trying this case."

"She just said she didn't care if she lived or died. And she wanted me to be her attorney. Also, she said all attorneys are the same. One as good as another."

George nodded his head. "I think you better be careful with this one. You say she's been diagnosed with borderline personality disorder? It's entirely possible that she's created some kind of a fantasy relationship with you in her head. That's just the kind of thing that would happen between a woman who is borderline and a guy like you who defended her and got her out of the mental institution before. You were her savior at that time. Her knight in shining armor. If you ask me, that's probably the main reason why she decided she wants you on her case."

I knew he was right and I didn't know what to do about it. "Maybe I should talk to James about the possibility of not being on this case. I mean, if she's imagining me to be her lover, her boyfriend, or whatever, that's not good. To say the very least."

"Well, it probably wouldn't hurt to bring it up with him. You gotta figure out, because it doesn't make any damn sense that she would have you on this case."

At that, I made another mental note to myself - I would have to talk to James. Hopefully he would realize the folly of keeping me on this case. And he would probably have to break it to her that she couldn't have me as an attorney.

Because, quite frankly, I didn't think I'd do good job.

Chapter Four

MARINA

MARINA WAS TAKEN BACK to her cell after she saw her lawyer and his investigator. She was happy she was able to pull it off. Aidan was unaware as to the reason why she wanted him on her case and what role he played in her life. And, she thought, it was probably how things had to be. She would never tell him the real reason why she wanted him as her attorney.

She felt a little bit sad that he was a dupe, a pawn in her scheme. He was an innocent guy, a boy really. He had no idea what he was getting into, and that was the way she wanted it to be.

Let him believe that the reason why she wanted him on her case was because she had some kind of an emotional attachment to him. Let him believe that, as his male ego would lead him to believe, that he was just That Good. Hell, let him even believe that she wanted him on the case because she wanted to lose. She didn't want to lose. She hated to lose anything.

Yet, in this case, losing might be the only way she could get what she wanted.

She only hoped that he could help her get out of this jail so she could do what she really wanted to do out in the world. She felt like a wild caged animal. She could feel the heat crawling from her insides, working its way through every cell in her body, so that her skin felt painful to the touch. She touched her arm, and it felt warm, like she had a severe fever.

She was sitting in her cell when her cellmate, Alyssa, came in. Alyssa was a mouse and Marina had no respect for her. Alyssa was in this place because she was caught with a bag of coke in her car. She told Marina that the coke didn't belong to her - it belonged to her boyfriend and she didn't know it was there. She was just driving his car because hers was in the shop. She was making a trip to Walmart when a cop pulled her over for a busted tail-light. She was nervous when he pulled her over, because cops, in general, freaked her out, and every time she was pulled over, she sweated bullets. Because she was so nervous, the cop asked her if she had been drinking. She said no, he made her walk the line and she blew clean. The cop then asked to search the car, and she let him. She didn't know the coke was underneath the mat in the backseat.

So she was genuinely shocked when the cop came to the window with the bag full of white powder, asked her about it, and then arrested her.

That wasn't what pissed Marina off. The girl was unlucky, that was all. No, what made Marina angry was that the bastard boyfriend, whose name was Greg, let Alyssa take the fall for him. He never even spoke to the prosecutors about who really owned those drugs. And yet, Alyssa was still crazy about him. That made Marina sick to her stomach.

Alyssa was scared all the time. She was one of those girls who cried herself to sleep every night and worried about what would happen to her. She walked around the lunch room like she was constantly worried that somebody would jump her, her tiny frame compacted even more than it already was, her eyes always darting around the room. Marina thought that Alyssa half expected a prison riot every single day, with her caught in the middle.

When Marina returned to her cell, Alyssa was on the top bunk, crying, as usual. She was also shaking all over. Marina rolled her eyes. She despised weak people.

Marina decided to play a trick on her wuss of a roommate. She was dying to do something that made her feel like she was alive, and tricking people was one of the ways she did it.

"I just saw my attorney and his investigator, and you'll never guess who I saw when I was meeting with him." Marina smiled, knowing that she was about to lie, and it was a lie that Alyssa could certainly catch her on if she had a brain in her pea head.

Obviously, she didn't see anybody else when she went to see her attorney, because her attorney had to meet with her in private. If there were other parties around when she talked to Aidan, there wouldn't be any kind of confidentiality in what she said to him. She knew enough about the law to know that this was true.

Alyssa turned her red-rimmed eyes to Marina and faced her. Her mousy brown hair was tangled and she had obviously not showered for quite a long time. Which was par for the course, because the girls didn't shower every day.

Alyssa's lips were quivering, and she was as tiny as a

bird. "Who?" she asked in a small voice. Her left hand went up to her neck and she looked like she was stroking a nonexistent necklace.

"Don't you know?" Marina asked casually. "Well, I'll give you one hint. I saw Gregory." Alyssa pined for Gregory the loser day after day, night after night. She had pictures of Gregory up on her wall and she confided in Marina that she was worried that he wasn't going to wait for her to serve her sentence for distribution. Apparently, the amount of coke in the car was enough that the prosecutors were able to charge her with intent to distribute, which means she probably was facing quite a few years in prison.

Marina was, quite frankly, disgusted by the whole thing. Here was a girl pining after a guy who let her take the fall for him. As far as Marina was concerned, Greg was lower than low.

So Marina felt she was doing Alyssa a favor when she said, "he was here to see somebody else. I think you probably know who I'm talking about. Jennifer, in the cell next to us."

Jennifer was a statuesque blonde, hot, a mean girl fully grown. Marina went on. "Greg and Jennifer were talking about how he couldn't wait to get her out of jail so that he could get her into his bed again. Or something like that. I don't know. All I know is that they were making googly eyes at each other the entire time."

Alyssa's eyes got huge, and her lips started to quiver even more. Marina was struck by how gullible Alyssa was. "He, he, he, he, was here to see Jennifer?" She started to breathe harder and harder. "Why was he seeing her?"

Marina rolled her eyes. "I just told you why he was seeing her. Apparently he and Jennifer are banging. And I even heard him say that he wasn't concerned about you because you're going to be going away for a long time for what he did. I think it's time for you to stop pining away for that guy, take the pictures down, and get on with it."

Marina felt powerful. She felt like she had Alyssa on her knees. Alyssa needed to just forget about that asshole Gregory, and come to her senses. If Alyssa wasn't going to come to her senses on her own, Marina would help her along.

When Marina went to bed that night, she didn't feel badly about her roommate crying herself to sleep. She cried herself to sleep anyhow, every night. She was wailing more than usual, however, and Marina had to put her pillow over her ears to drown out the noise.

Chapter Five

BY 2 AM, Marina's thoughts had changed. As she heard her cellmate crying, she felt extremely guilty. She felt like such a terrible person. Sometimes she had a hard time looking at herself in the mirror, knowing what kind of an ugly person she was inside and out. Alyssa was an innocent soul who believed anything. Marina felt awful about dropping the lie about Gregory on her. That was a hammer that should never have dropped.

There were times when she felt so bad about herself that she wanted to take her own life. Just end it all. She had a hard time dealing with the pain, the psychic pain that came from growing up in a Russian orphanage where she was starved, beaten, chained to a bed night and day, and sexually abused. That was why she delighted in making other people hurt - she, herself, was in severe pain, and sometimes the only way to lessen that pain was to visit it on somebody else. It was almost like she was able to give another person her own pain, if only for a moment, and, for that moment, she felt her own pain just a little bit less.

However, when she heard Alyssa wailing that night, at first, she was annoyed. Then she felt terribly guilty.

She didn't do things like this. Wicked Marina did. She didn't. She tended to think there is a part of herself that was almost like a demon, one that could never be sated. A demon that wanted to destroy everything. One that wanted to watch the world burn, like the Joker in Batman.

She hated when the demon would come out. Not that she could ever keep it in, because it just came out whenever it wanted to. She had seen many psychotherapists over the years because she desperately wanted to know how to cope with life. One of her psychotherapists asked her to give a name to her demon, and treat her demon as if she would a friend. Try to talk to her kindly and try to reason with her.

So, Marina initially named her demon Sarah. Marina imagined Sarah to be a white bread girl, calm and soothing. Sarah was a girl who lived in a beautiful home up in Encinitas, maybe, or maybe Del Mar, or La Jolla, where Marina lived. Sarah was somebody who never cheated on her husband, who never would have lied to an innocent like Alyssa, who never would have physically attacked her own attorney. Sarah would have been kind to Aidan, respectful, honest. That was the kind of person Sarah was, and that's the kind of person Marina wished her demon was.

But her demon wasn't like that. No, Marina's demon was named something else - Malphas, second in command to Satan in hell. That was how Marina saw her evil self. Malphas was the bad Marina, her shadow self.

Marina almost thought sometimes that her demon, Malphus or Sarah, depending on Marina's mood, was a separate person from her. The demon had different appetites, both sexually and food. For instance, Malphus could not tolerate milk. Marina loved dairy. Malphus loved hot foods, such as ghost peppers and other kinds of hot peppers such as habaneros. Marina was convinced that Malphus liked to consume those foods because it made Marina's insides burn. It made Marina have the runs that chafed when it came out and caused a rash. It gave Marina severe indigestion.

Malphus enjoyed torturing, psychologically, people around her, and also enjoyed physically torturing people who got in her way. And yet, whenever Malphus wreaked havoc on the people around her, Marina was never able to quite apologize for the way she acted.

And she didn't know why.

Malphus was a horrible person. She was sadistic, cruel, and manipulative. Malphus made Marina sick, yet Marina knew that Malphus was a part of her and always would be.

The question was, did Malphus somehow come out on the night of her husband's murder? Sometimes she thought that Malphus would take over her body, which was why she had such losses of time.

She knew that when she saw her attorney again, the poor sap by the name of Aidan, she would probably be back to Malphus, the mean, shadow side of her self. As much as she didn't want that to happen, there was no controlling it.

She wished she could warn Aidan about what he was getting into, but she couldn't.

Because she knew she would not be herself by the time she saw him again.

Chapter Six

AIDAN

REGINA MET me at my law office on Monday morning. I'd already made it clear to James that I wanted her to be my investigator, explaining to him that our investigators were not experienced in investigating murder trials, and Regina was. They agree to go ahead and contract with her, paying her $200 per hour. Regina was happy with that.

"Okay, who's first on our agenda, as far as who we're going to talk to?" Regina asked me. She had her boots up on my desk and was leaning back in her chair. She was dressed in a leather jacket and a tight red shirt that showed off her impressive curves. As usual, she took my breath away.

"Well, I was hoping I could to send you off to track down some leads. I have to go to court for Marina today. She's having her arraignment and bond review hearing. I think I can probably get her a bond, but it's going to be pretty steep – $5 million or more. But I think she can afford to pay that."

"So, have you decided that you're going to try to figure out if this chick did it or not?" Regina asked.

"Obviously. I mean, I have to cover all my bases with this woman. Because, as you say, getting a not guilty by reason of insanity verdict won't be a walk in the park. Especially because we don't even know if she did it or not. So I need to track down some of the people they corresponded with over the Internet. People they invited into their bedroom."

"What are you talking about?" Regina asked.

"I found out Lawrence and Marina had an open marriage and found people to swing with on a site called Alt.com," I said. "It's a site where people find others who like to play. I had Christian get the records of all the people they contacted on this site, and there were quite a few people, so I hope you don't get too bogged down in this. Just collect their backgrounds, see who might have criminal records, find out who has any signs of violence in their past. Maybe a restraining order or two along the way. From what Christian tells me, it doesn't seem like they were exactly discriminating about who they hung out with. Maybe when you can talk to them, they can give you some leads as to who else we can track down. That's where I want you to start."

"So, you're thinking a rando they picked up might have done him in?"

"Well, let's start there. We have to start somewhere."

"Will do." Regina took the list of people out of my hand and took a look at it. She nodded. "I see some familiar names on here from my own days of being a working girl. Thank you for this Aidan, this will be helpful."

I nodded and looked at her. I wanted to say something else to her. I wanted to see if she wanted to go out that night, but the way she shot me down the other day, I knew I was gun shy.

"Well, hopefully you can try to figure something out from this list," I finally said.

She took the list and left without a word.

And I got ready to go to court for my client.

Chapter Seven

REGINA

REGINA HAD LOOKED through the list of people she was given by Aidan and wasn't feeling hopeful about it. She had a nagging feeling there was something she and Aidan weren't seeing and she didn't really know what it was.

She had a feeling she'd be barking up the wrong tree with these people. But she would be game about it anyway.

She managed to find one guy on the list, his name was Brock, who had multiple restraining orders against him. He was somebody brought into Marina and Lawrence's relationship as a part-time player, at least that was what she gathered from the evidence. The cell phone records that Christian had managed to get showed they'd called this guy several times over the course of six months, and, since he was known to be a violent person – at least he was according to his girlfriend, Daniela Thompson – Regina would start with him first.

She made an appointment to see him and then went over to his apartment. He was living in Barrio Logan, not exactly the most high class neighborhood in the area, and his apartment complex was extremely rundown. It was one of those apartment complexes that was probably built in the 1950s and not updated since then. All the cars in the parking lot were older model, with exception of just a few, and Regina knew she was probably going to come across more than a few condoms and broken bottles in the parking lot, so she would have to be careful.

She gingerly stepped along the sidewalk, passing by discarded potato chip wrappers and bottles filled with a yellow liquid that she knew was not Mountain Dew, and got to a heavy steel door. Opening the door, which opened into the stairway, she was hit in the face with the stench of rotting food and piss.

She walked up the six flights of stairs to where his floor was. As she walked down the hallway, she heard babies crying in multiple apartments, and, in one apartment, she heard the loud sounds of people having sex, and right next to that the even louder sounds of a major fight between a man and a woman. The man was screaming at the woman and the woman was crying. And because the walls were so thin, Regina heard all of it.

Brock's apartment was at the end of the hall. The carpet in the hallway was threadbare, and in certain areas, it was completely see-through. Like that stairway, it smelled of urine and rotting garbage. She thought she smelled something else and then saw down the hallway that there was a dead rat laying next to the wall. He'd been decomposing for quite a while, judging by the looks of it, and the stench of the rotting animal amplified all the other smells. Regina felt herself wanting to gag.

She knocked on the door. She wondered how somebody like this Brock person, who obviously had no money, could hook up with such high-rollers as Marina and her husband Lawrence.

She heard of slumming before, but this was something else entirely.

Brock opened the door. He was expecting her, but, by the looks of it, he didn't want company at all. He was wearing a stained wife-beater and boxer shorts. His legs were extremely pale. He had a shock of bright red hair, the color of Marina's, and the hairs on his legs were the same color, except for more ginger. He was extremely skinny, his face long and gaunt. When he smiled, she noticed several missing teeth. And the few teeth he had in his head were rotting out.

"Brock Lewis?" Regina asked him.

"Yeah. I guess you're Regina, huh? You wanted to talk to me about Lawrence and Marina, huh?"

"Yeah, that's right," Regina said.

He invited her in and she stepped into the apartment and looked around. As with the hallway, the carpet was threadbare and extremely cheap. It was a sickly color of green and was thin as paper.

He had a cat, an enormous orange monstrosity that was pooping in the litter box as she walked in. The poor cat didn't have any kind of toys around - no scratching posts, no towers to sit in.

For that matter, Brock didn't have a place for Regina to sit either. There was a chair, but only one, and it had an enormous hole in the the middle of it. It looked like something that someone probably had thrown out on the curb and this guy picked it up and brought it into his apartment for himself. Other than that chair, though, there was no furniture in the place where Regina could sit. Besides the chair, the only furniture in the place consisted of a chest of drawers, which, like the leather chair, looked like it had seen better days. The paint was peeling off of it and the middle door was completely missing. On top of the dresser was an old-school television, the kind with the glass front and large back, like people watched in the 1980s. The kind you could find on Craigslist for free any day the week.

Brock looked embarrassed. "Here, sit in my chair. I'll just sit here on the floor. You can ask me any question you want to ask me."

This wasn't right. Something was very off about this entire scenario.

Lawrence was a billionaire, for the love of God. Regina thought a guy like him would probably get his freak on with wealthy strange people, just like him. Regina thought rich people preferred to hang with people like them. The rich people on ALT.com would attract other rich people. They wouldn't be attracting a toothless wonder living in a little slum like this Brock person was.

"Yeah, I'd like to ask you about a couple of people you've been hooking up with over the past few months. Lawrence Murphy and his wife Marina Vasiliev."

Brock smiled. He was sitting on the floor next to Regina, who was leaning back in the leather recliner that was apparently taken off the street somewhere. It wasn't the most comfortable recliner in the entire world, considering it not only had a hole going down the middle of it, but the back cushion was so worn down that she could feel the springs jabbing into her spine. Not that she really cared about that. She wasn't exactly somebody who had to have comfort at all times. She was anything but. But she still thought it was very strange that this individual knew two people like Marina and Lawrence.

"Yeah, they're a lot of fun," Brock said.

"What did you do with them?"

"I sold them drugs." And he smiled his toothless smile. "Oh I know you actually got my name from some of the people they were hooking up with on alt.com. Listen, I put certain codewords into my profile that told anybody who was looking at me what I really wanted to do. They weren't swinging with me. I can almost guarantee that."

Regina was still confused. Maybe this guy was a drug dealer, she thought, but he couldn't have been a very good one. He was obviously broke. If somebody sold drugs to a rich guy like Lawrence and his wife, he certainly wouldn't be staying in a slum like this.

"Nice try. What did you really do with them?" Regina asked.

"What do you mean?" he asked. "You don't believe me?"

"No. I don't believe you. I'm sorry, I hate to be blunt, but that's kind of the way I roll. You are not a high-powered drug dealer. If you were, you wouldn't be living here. You would have had your teeth fixed. You would've showered in the past week or so and I would hazard a guess that the reason why you haven't showered is probably because your shower isn't working. You probably have called your supervisor time and time again about it and he refuses to do anything about it. How close am I?"

The smile never left the guy's face. "Okay, you got me."

"So how did you really know Lawrence and Marina?" Regina asked. "That's the question of the day. What were they to you? I refuse to believe you were hooking up with them for either sex or drugs. So what gives? How did you know them?"

At this point, the guy's smile finally left his face. "What do you want to know about Marina and

Lawrence?" he asked without answering her earlier question.

"You know what happened to Lawrence, don't you?" Regina asked him.

"Of course. Somebody shot him in the face three times. Marina was arrested for the murder, I mean I just know about this because this is what I read about in the paper."

"So are you telling me you didn't know about the murder except for what you read in the paper?" Regina asked.

"That's exactly what I'm telling you," he said. "I was not that close with them."

"Listen, I don't know what kind of game you think you're playing here," Regina said impatiently. "I asked you a question earlier and I would like an answer to it. Lawrence and Regina have been contacting you on your profile on alt.com for the past six months. You and I both know you're probably not their type. Not sexually and not as a drug hook up, either. I'm going to hazard a guess that you probably have no visible means of income, except for maybe welfare or disability."

Regina thought that she might've been onto something. Maybe the guy was mentally disabled and he knew Marina from the mental institution. That would actually make a lot of sense, one hell of a lot more sense than that he actually knew them some other way. She felt sorry for the guy, in a way, but at the same time, she was getting impatient with his obvious lying.

"What makes you think I don't have any visible means of income, besides disability?" he asked

"Isn't it obvious?" Regina shot back. "Listen, the reason why I'm talking to you is because I thought there was a possibility that you were hooking up with these two and you know something. Maybe you knew there was some kind of a jealous lover's quarrel or something of the sort. Maybe you wanted kill him and you knew Marina and Lawrence were fighting, so you knew you could frame her. Maybe you had something against both of them. Killing him and framing her would be the perfect mode of revenge. Wouldn't it?" She was shooting in the dark and she knew it, but, still, she watched him carefully for his reaction to her accusations.

Regina was disappointed when he simply said "yes, I suppose it would be. I suppose it would be at that."

But that was all he said. He wouldn't commit to anything else and Regina knew it.

She was still extremely curious as to exactly how he knew these two and would have a keep him in mind. After all, he apparently was violent, judging from the fact that he had restraining orders against him. So she would have to keep him at the top of her list of people who she would have to follow up on.

She decided to press him a little bit more. "Listen, I don't know what kind of game you're playing. And quite frankly, I don't really care. I just want to know if there's anything you know about these two that you can tell me. Anything at all."

He rocked a little bit on the floor next to her, the smile never leaving his face. It was almost creepy the way he smiled. He certainly didn't have a reason to smile at that moment. Regina was pressing him and he could possibly have been in trouble. But it didn't matter to him, apparently. Because he just kept smiling.

"No, there's not much I can really tell you about them."

"Okay then. I'm going to keep you on my list, however. And I would appreciate it if you could tell me if there's anybody else I should talk to about Lawrence's murder."

He shook his head a bit. "And how do you know he was murdered?"

What kind of question was that? "Because he was shot in the face three times. Of course he was murdered. Why would you even ask that question?"

"Are you saying he definitely was shot in the face three times? You got the ballistics report?"

Regina had to admit she'd not yet gotten a hold of the file for this case. She'd ordered it and it wasn't like her to not get the file before talking to witnesses, which was her first mistake. A rookie mistake. She hadn't seen the ballistics report and had only heard Lawrence was shot three times in the face through the media. Did the media get it wrong? That wouldn't be unheard of.

"What are you saying?" Regina asked.

He just shrugged. "I'm not saying anything. Although I will tell you that I knew the two of them. They didn't get along very well. I'm sure Marina probably said something about the fights. Right?"

"Yes, of course she talked about the fights. But maybe you can tell me a little more about them?"

"All I know is what she told me. She confided in me. She told me had terrible fights where he would beat on her. He was very controlling. According to Marina, he didn't want her to do anything outside the house, really. He definitely didn't want her to work. He had a hard time with her even going out with her friends. He isolated her. You know, like an abuser would. And I don't really know if he was abusing her, but I do know that he made her feel like she was a prisoner in her own home."

Regina watched Brock while he spoke. There was something off about his body language. About the way he just kept smiling when he was talking about the supposed emotional and physical abuse that Marina was going through at the hands of Lawrence. Regina was very good at reading people and she thought he was probably lying.

Why he was lying, she didn't know. It was like he was covering for her.

Why would he be covering for her? She still didn't know exactly what relationship he had with the two of them. But it seemed there was a possibility he was closer with her than she was with him.

"I see." Regina narrowed her eyes. "That's not how I understood things to be. I know she wasn't working, but she had friends. She went out with them, sometimes a lot. She wasn't isolated at all. So why would you say she was?"

He just shrugged. "Listen, I'm just trying to blow smoke up your butt. I didn't really know those two. Not at all. I just wanted to give you a good story and I suppose that was good as any. But I think you need to talk to somebody else."

"Okay, could you give me any names of people I should talk to?"

He just chuckled a little. "I'll be sure and get back with you if I can figure that out. In the meantime, I really have to get to work." He motioned over to a computer on a card table in the corner of the room. The computer was so old that it still had the old-school monitor – a glass face with the large cone of hard plastic behind it. It wasn't a flatscreen like a modern monitor.

He looked over at that computer and Regina looked over at him. "I got it off the curb," he said. "What can I say, I can't afford much of anything."

"What do you do on that computer?" Regina asked.

"I do surveys online. It's all I do. And they don't pay much at all. And as you can probably tell, I live off the government dime. Disability."

"Can I ask what your disability is?" Regina asked.

"You're a smart person. You can probably figure out what my disability is. If you figure that out, you can probably figure out how I know Marina. Now, really, I'd like you to leave."

Regina felt stupid. Of course! He probably knew Marina through one of her stays in the hospital.

"Are you mentally ill?" Regina point-blank asked him.

He shook his head and smiled.

"No. I've not been diagnosed with mental illness. At least not yet."

He was speaking in riddles and Regina didn't like it. "Okay, dude. I guess this is where I leave you. Although, as I said, I won't necessarily let you off the hook. I'm going to try to figure out what's going on and I might come back to talk to you some more. So don't go too far. That's all I'm asking."

"Okay. I won't."

Regina left the stinking apartment and made her way to her car, which she was afraid would get jacked in his neighborhood.

That guy was extremely odd. To say the very least. And nothing he told her made sense. It all seemed to be either a lie or just plain nonsensical.

At the same time, deep down, Regina knew there was something familiar about that guy. Like she'd seen him before, although she knew she hadn't.

So why did she get the feeling of déjà vu?

And what was all that about him being disabled and that somehow was associated with Marina?

Or maybe it was associated with Lawrence?

Whatever it was, Regina knew she'd have to try to figure it out.

Chapter Eight

AIDAN

WHEN I GOT to the jail, I saw Marina walking in with the other inmates. Their wrists were shackled together, one to the other. They moved as one over to the cubicle were they would address the judge from behind a bulletproof glass. A guard unlocked them, but they still had their hands shackled together, even though they were now individuals, not just part of one large mass of people.

"You going to get me out of this joint?" Marina asked me.

"I'll try. I think I can. The prosecutor's telling me he'll ask for a $5 million bond, and it looks like the judge will probably go along with it. I think you have that kind of money, don't you?"

She snorted. "Well, let me see. I was married to my husband for the past eight years. He gave me a million dollars a year. And I never spent that money, because I lived off him all this time. So, yeah, you're in luck. I have that kind of money. You think you can actually get it done?"

"I wouldn't say it to you if I didn't think it was doable. I wouldn't get your hopes up like that."

Marina nodded. "My roommate Alyssa killed herself last night." She smiled. "You ever hear a rumor in college where they said that if your roommate killed herself during the school year that you'd get automatic A's in all your classes? They even made some kind of movie about it, you know. Some kind of horror flick."

I had a laugh about that. Yes, that was a story that went around my college, just like with everyone else's college. I went to UCLA, and, just like Regina was talking about, there was a story that if one's roommate committed suicide during the year, that person would get an automatic free pass throughout all his or her classes. Automatic A's. I never believed it and knew it was some kind of bullshit urban legend. But I wondered what she was getting at.

"Yeah, I heard about that. Why?"

"Well, my cellmate died. She hanged herself from a bed sheet. I saw her do it. I don't know why they gave her a bedsheet the first place, but I guess they probably wanted her to hang herself. What can I say. Anyhow, I'm traumatized. I think you should ask the judge if I could just go free because of the trauma of seeing my cellmate off herself like that."

Just then, one of Marina's jail mates, a girl by the name of Sabrina, with dirty blonde hair, a washed-out complexion, and pox all over her face, piped in. "She shouldn't get any kind of favors, because she's the one who made her cellmate kill herself. Telling her that lie about her boyfriend. What kind of person are you?"

Marina just shrugged. "Hey, I was doing her a favor. That guy's a tool, to say the very least. I mean, he let her take the fall for his bullshit? What kind of guy is that? She deserved so much better. I was just trying to get her away from him."

"No you weren't. You didn't care if Alyssa was involved with a guy who was using her. You just wanted to hurt her. And that's just the way you are. Just want to just hurt people. The weaker they are, the more you want to twist the knife. You twisted that knife so hard that she couldn't stand it."

Marina just smiled at me. "You're looking extremely handsome today. Who's your tailor?"

I looked down at my suit, which was charcoal gray and fit like a glove. The one thing I really wanted to do when I got this job was to look extremely sharp, so I didn't go to Men's Warehouse to get my clothes - I went to Nordstrom's, Neiman Marcus, Bloomingdale's. I found a personal shopper who made sure everything was tailored just-so. Part of me was happy that she noticed my suit, but part of me also knew she was just saying stuff to me because she wanted to butter me up. She probably didn't want me to ask her questions about the death of her poor cellmate.

"I don't have a tailor. Listen, tell me about this Alyssa chick. What really happened with her?"

"I don't know. All I know is that I told her a few white lies about her boyfriend, who caused her to be in jail in the first place. The next thing I know, she's hanging from the top bunk. It wasn't my fault that happened. It was the fault of the jail for letting her have a bedsheet in the first place. She should've been under suicide watch after she found out her boyfriend was banging somebody else."

I was confused. "I thought you said the story you told her about her boyfriend was a lie?"

Marina's green eyes seemed to darken, although I was sure I was just imagining that. She blinked a few times, and then she smiled. "Do you believe everything I tell you?" she purred sweetly. "Now listen, I told you two different things. You obviously have to believe one of them, don't you? Do you believe that I lied to her about her boyfriend, or do you believe I told her the truth about her boyfriend and she just didn't want to hear it? Which do you believe?"

I looked over at Sabrina, who was shaking her head. "Don't fall for it. Nothing that comes out of this woman's mouth is the truth."

"That's not true," Marina said. "I do tell the truth. I also tell a lot of lies. It's up to you to try to determine which is which. If you can do that, you'll have no problem at all defending me. Now, back to my original question. Which story do you believe about Alyssa?"

"I'm not playing your games," I said. "I'm your attorney, and just as sure as I'm on your case, I can withdraw from it. In fact, I'd like to."

"No, you cannot withdraw from my case," she said. "You don't think I know James gave you this case and if you decide to drop me as your client, James will fire you? He will, you know. You'll be out on the street tomorrow. Of course, a guy as gorgeous as you would have absolutely no problem finding another job, but I think you like this one. And I think you don't want to admit it, but I think you like me. I think you like me like you like that other girl, that Regina girl that came in with you. I think you just don't want to admit it, though. Sad, really."

While Marina was talking, there was something very uncomfortable stirring inside me. That was the one thing I'd always learned about people with borderline personality disorder. They can be extremely seductive. Charming. You always had to watch your back with them, because if you didn't, there would soon be a knife protruding from it.

"No, actually, I think of you just as another client."

I looked at Marina, and I noticed she was breathing very heavily, in and out of her nose and mouth.

"You leave me, and you'll see what happens to you," she said in a tone of voice that almost made me think she was possessed by something. It was a strange, like Mercedes McCambridge's voice coming out of little Linda Blair in *The Exorcist*.

She scared me just a little, but I had to avoid that fear. "I will leave you if you're not straight with me," I said.

Now her voice was tiny, fleeting. She seemed to shrink down in her seat, becoming smaller and smaller. It was like Alice after she drank the potion that made her tiny. "Please. Please, I'll do anything. Don't leave me. I'll be good. I promise. I'm so sorry. Please don't leave me."

I looked over at Sabrina, who was watching the entire scene unfold with a small smile on her face.

"I wouldn't let her manipulate you if I were you," Sabrina said with a sneer on her face. "That's the best way to get sucked into her games. And that's what they are. Games. Nothing more than that."

Just then, I heard on the other side of the glass that the judge was calling Marina's case. I entered my appearance and asked for a bond reduction. At the moment, the bond was set at $10 million, and Marina had indicated to me that she only had $8 million in the bank. If the bond wasn't lowered, obviously Marina couldn't bond out.

I was lucky that the prosecutor, Jenna Powell, didn't have any objections to my request, and, before I knew it, the judge was setting the case for a case management date and lowering the bond to $5 million.

"Your honor," I said. "I would like to defer the formal arraignment for another time. I would like some time with this case so that I can determine if I would like to plea my client not guilty or not guilty by reason of insanity."

The judge nodded. "Ms. Redford, any objections to that?" she asked.

"No, your honor," Jenna said.

"Okay, then, Mr. Collins, I'll continue the formal arraignment for two weeks from today," the judge said.

"Actually, I'd also like to schedule this case for a hearing on whether or not my client is competent to stand trial," I said. "I'd like to get this determination before we proceed to a formal arraignment."

Judge Watts nodded her head. "Very well, I'll schedule the competency hearing for two weeks from today." Then she looked over at her assistant, who gave Jenna and me dates for our next hearing.

"Thank you," Marina said humbly, bowing her head. It seemed that it was the other Marina I'd managed to meet that day, the shy one that shrunk down in her chair and tried to become invisible. "I don't know how to thank you for getting me out of this place."

"I'm only doing my job."

"And so you are. Well, I guess I can be taken back to the jail and I'll be out soon. I'll be walking out of the jail with just the clothes on my back. I was wondering if you could give me a ride to my home in La Jolla?"

I wanted to protest. I had things to do that night. I really didn't want to have to drive her from the jail to her house in La Jolla. Yet, just the way that she looked at me, I knew I'd be doing it.

"Of course. I'll do that."

But I wondered one thing after I made the commitment to drive her home.

Which Marina would be talking to me that night?

Chapter Nine

THAT MONDAY, I received the interrogation reel from the prosecutor's office. I had requested it because I wanted to see how Marina acted when she was questioned.

It was disturbing, to say the least.

"Ms. Vasiliev," Officer Ryan said to her on the grainy footage. "Do you know why you're here?"

She nodded her head. "Yes. I was bad."

"Tell me about that. Why do you say you were bad?"

"I ate a cookie when my mother told me not to. She told me that it would spoil my dinner, but I didn't care. I wanted that cookie, so I ate it."

Officer Ryan shook his head. "Ms. Vasiliev, you were at your house just now when we found your husband. You were in a chair in the living room while your husband was shot dead in the foyer. What happened to your husband?"

"My mother is mad at me. She's going to ground me for that cookie. It's unfair. She told me it was the principal, not the act. I have to follow her rules or pay the price. But it was only a cookie. Nobody else gets grounded for eating cookies."

I could see Officer Ryan visibly getting agitated. "Ms. Vasiliev, do you know how your husband ended up dead?"

"The tin man did it," she said, nodding her head. "He needed a heart. Yet he got sad when he thought he was losing his friends. He had a heart. And the scarecrow needed a brain, but he was always the one coming up with the good ideas. He didn't need a brain, he had one."

And so it went. Officer Ryan kept asking her questions, and she kept answering in *non-sequiturs*. This went on for several hours. Different officers kept coming in and out, asking her questions, and she kept answering these questions in a bizarre way.

Either she was really dissociating or she's a damned good actress.

The problem was, I didn't know which one of those scenarios were true.

Chapter Ten

SINCE I WASN'T sure if I would go with NGRI or plead Marina just straight not guilty, I would have to get more information about her mental illness. So I made an appointment with her treating doctor.

The doctor who'd been treating her for the past several years was named Dr. Alan. He was a fiftyish man with gray hair, a goatee, and a slight build - about 5'6", a buck forty, more or less. He'd been practicing in the field of psychotherapy for the past 30 years and had been treating her for the past 10. I made an appointment to see him and made sure to go over to Marina's house and get a waiver signed so I could speak with him.

That was an interesting experience, to say the very least.

I called her on the phone and told her what I needed. She invited me to come over to her house. When I got there, she was dressed in a tiny see-through négligée. I could see every bit of her skin underneath it. She was wearing some kind of perfume. I couldn't really describe it, except that it smelled of flowers, woods and spices. All kinds of spices. She was wearing full make up, her blue eyes brighter than usual. Her full lips were dressed in red lipstick.

Her house was in La Jolla, a tony city just north of San Diego, and it was one of those enormous 5,000 square-foot mansions, all Spanish architecture with porticos, arches, a large swimming pool out back and a roof made out of Spanish-style clay pots.

The lawn was perfectly manicured and there was a guesthouse in the back. The interior of the house sported high ceilings, hardwood floors, stained glass, and chandeliers. She led me over to a room where there was an enormous fireplace, and a fire blazing, even though it was June and there was no need for a fire to be blazing at all. The room also had floor-to-ceiling windows and was framed by an enormous arch.

"Now, you were telling me on the phone that you want me to sign some kind of a paper?" she asked me.

"Yeah. I need you to sign a waiver so I can speak with your psychotherapist, Dr. Alan."

"Why do you need to speak with Dr. Alan?" she asked.

"Well, as I said, I want to try to plead you not guilty by reason of insanity," I said.

I would have to decide quickly if I wanted to go down the insanity route. The judge gave me two weeks to make my decision. After Marina's arraignment, I had a short conference with the judge in his chambers, and he told me that he wanted me to not only have Marina evaluated for the insanity defense, but also to see if she was even fit to stand trial for her crime.

My research on the matter of whether or not Marina was fit for trial was mixed on the issue of amnesia and whether or not that made a person unfit for trial. Some of the case law stated that amnesia about the crime in question meant the accused couldn't help counsel and couldn't assist in her own defense. According to the Constitution, the accused must be able to consult with her lawyer with a reasonable degree of rational understanding of what she's accused of doing. According to what Marina said to me, she didn't really have that kind of capacity, because she had no real knowledge of how her husband died.

Granted, there was also case law on the other side of the question, as many courts stated that amnesia was not a reason a person can be declared to be incompetent to stand trial. Even so, I knew there was a chance that Marina could be declared incompetent to be tried and I had to try for that declaration.

So the judge scheduled a hearing to determine if Marina was fit to stand trial. And then, once that was ruled upon, the judge scheduled another arraignment for her, where I could plead her not guilty by reason of insanity. That was the way the judge decided when I explained what was happening.

So the first thing I needed to do was talk to Marina's psychotherapist. And I explained all this to her.

"Well, the reason why I need to talk with him is because I need to ask him about your dissociative states. I'm doing some research on this entire issue of not guilty by reason of insanity. In California the standard they follow is called the M'Naghten rule. Do you know what that is?"

"Of course, darling." She batted her eyes at me. I thought she was acting very strange, because her behavior was so different from the way she acted the first time around. "The rule is that the person doesn't understand what she did. Or she does know what she did but didn't know that it was wrong. I'd imagine that what you're going to try to do is tell the jury that I didn't know what I did. Because I know murder is wrong. I'm not that crazy."

"That's right," I said. I was impressed that Marina knew as much about the M'Naghten rule as she did. "Obviously, I'll tell the jury you had no idea what you were doing when you killed him."

She shook her head. "Listen, I thought we went through this. I know we talked about this. Just the other day."

Right before my eyes, her face changed. When I first arrived at her house to talk with her, she had an almost innocent look on her face. Her eyes were wide, her face was open. She looked almost like a child who was wanting to please her parents.

When I talked about the insanity plea, she changed. She narrowed her eyes and her face became like a stone. Hard, cold, unforgiving. The way her expression and facial features changed in an instance gave me chills, and not the good kind.

"Aidan, I know you don't want to lose your license to practice law. But that will happen if you don't do everything I'm asking you to do. I have a way of, shall I say, getting what I want."

I didn't know what she was talking about, but it didn't sound good.

"What are you talking about? I'm not going to lose my license to practice law just because I'm going against my client's wishes. And if you don't follow what I want to do with this case, how I want to try it, then it's really just a matter of me withdrawing from your case. I don't need this headache."

She cocked her head a little bit. Then she licked her lips. "Would you like a glass of wine?" she asked.

"No. I'm sorry. I'm on the job and I really don't want to mess things up."

I was feeling uncomfortable in her house. It was the way she was dressed, the way she was looking at me. It was like she was wanting to seduce me. Having a glass of wine with her would only encourage her, and that was the last thing I wanted to do.

"One glass. It's a bottle I got up in Temecula at a winery up there. Have you been up there?"

"No, I can't say I've been to Temecula."

That was a lie, of course. I lived in San Diego. Of course I'd been to Temecula. That was where the wineries were because grapes grew well in its fertile soil. I'd been up there with buddies and dates and it was always a fun time. But I wanted to cut off casual conversation with Marina, which was why I decided to lie and tell her I'd never been up there.

"Well, then, you're in for a treat," she said, her face soft again. It was as if she were trying everything, all her bags of tricks, to manipulate me. Start out being warm, move on to threats, and, when all else fails, get me drunk and try to seduce me. I was determined that all her games weren't going to work. *Just stop. You aren't going to get me off my strategy here.*

"Listen, as I said, we at least have to get the ball rolling on the insanity defense," I said, ignoring her entreaties about the wine. "Granted, if new evidence comes up at a later date where we can show you didn't actually do it, then I can talk to the judge about changing your plea to not guilty, as opposed to not guilty by reason of insanity. I spoke with some other attorneys about this very situation, and that's what they advised. But I have to preserve your plea of not guilty by reason of insanity by the next arraignment.

And this is assuming the judge finds you're competent to stand trial. So I have to talk to your psychotherapist and get all the information about your mental illness."

Marina took a deep breath, and it looked like she wasn't going to try any more tricks for the time being. I wondered if I was reading her right.

"Okay. Listen, tell me again about what my amnesia means for this case?" she asked.

"We have to show you did not have the *mens rea* for a crime. *Mens rea* means you have the mental intention to commit the crime. According to the research on the insanity defense and amnesia, if you had dissociation at the time of the crime and your dissociation was because of a recognized mental defect, we can probably plead insanity. There's no guarantee the judge would even accept an insanity plea unless I can show that. So it's very important that I get the records, and talk to your shrink, so he can tell me about your dissociations and about the reasons why you have these dissociative episodes."

She nodded. "Okay. I'll sign this piece of paper so you can talk to my doctor."

I was still suspicious of her, even after she signed the paper. She got properly dressed and we went to a law office to grab one of their notaries so that the waiver was official, and, the whole time I was with her, I was waiting for the other shoe to drop. I was waiting for Marina to show me one of her many other faces, but she didn't.

After she signed the waiver, I headed downtown to see her shrink, Dr. Alan.

Chapter Eleven

WHEN I GOT to Dr. Alan's office suite, his secretary led me into his office and I sat down on the leather couch right in front of his desk. Dr. Alan's office was the kind of office I'd like to be in if my head was being shrunk. The floors were hardwood, with colorful throw rugs all around. His furniture was modern, with a glass desk, modern art on the walls and big leather chairs and sofas. He had an alcove in between two enormous book shelves that were filled with books about psychiatry and psychology, and the alcove had an exposed stone backsplash that I really thought was eye-catching. What I really liked, however, was how much light was pouring in through the room through floor-to-ceiling low-e glass windows.

Dr. Alan was staring at some fish in his tank when I walked in the door. He looked up at me as he fed them. "Aidan Collins, I presume?" he asked me.

"Yes, that's me. I called you on the phone earlier and made an arrangement to meet with you about a patient."

He nodded. "Yes. I know you want to talk to me about

Marina Vasiliev. It's a sad thing, what happened with her. That she's accused of murdering her husband. It's a tragic thing."

"Yes, it is," I agreed. "I need to talk with you about her background. As you probably know, there are two hurdles I have to clear with the court. One is that I need a determination if she's competent to stand trial. Because, as you know, she doesn't remember the night her husband died so she doesn't know if she killed him or if she didn't, so she's not really able to assist me with her own defense. I'm sure you're aware that in the state of California, simply not remembering a crime doesn't necessarily mean you can't stand trial for it, but I need to at least make that argument.

"Yes, yes, of course," Dr. Alan said, nodding. He had finally turned away from his fish feeding duties and he was sitting behind his desk, staring at his clasped hands.

I went on. "The other argument is that even if she does stand trial, I need to possibly plead her not guilty by reason of insanity. That's where you come in. According to my research, if a person dissociates, and the dissociation occurred at the time of the crime and was part a long-standing mental disease, I could plead her guilty by reason of insanity. So I need to find out more about her personality disorder and her dissociative states."

He nodded again and then stood up and sat down on top of the desk. Which was odd, but, at the same time, it was comforting that he could be so casual.

"Okay," he began. "Marina is fractured. That's the best way to describe what she's going through. She has all the classic signs of an individual with borderline personality disorder. She's terrified of being abandoned. When she cares about somebody, if she thinks that person is going to leave her, she gets frantic, even paranoid. She has an intense fear of that. But at the same time, she sometimes tries to pretend she doesn't need anybody."

"Did you think that maybe Lawrence was about to leave her?" That was one possibility, I had to admit. Maybe Lawrence wanted to leave and Marina got so frantic that she killed him.

He shook his head. "No. I don't think he was going to leave her. Marina and Lawrence, they had a complicated relationship, but I really received the impression from speaking with her that the relationship with her husband wasn't close. She didn't attach to him the way you might think a person with borderline personality disorder would attach to her husband. She thought of him as an object. A means to an end. I hope that makes sense."

I thought about what she told me about Lawrence, and about how he essentially paid her to be married to him. Which I still thought was odd.

"So do you think it was more like a business arrangement between her and Lawrence, then?" I asked Dr. Alan.

"Yes. That's exactly what I thought about her relationship with him. As far as I know, she didn't have any real attachments. But I did note there was a friend of hers, her name was Celia, and I guess Celia and she grew up together. As you know, Marina has only been in this country since the age of seven. Before she was seven, she was in an orphanage in Russia and she experienced terrible things there. When she came to this country, she was adopted by a family, Celeste and Tommy Williams. They gave her anything she could ask for. Including love, and Celeste even stayed home with her. But, unfortunately, because Marina spent her formative years in an orphanage being sexually abused, neglected, starved, beaten and tied to a bed half the time, and not getting the kind of attachments she needed with another adult, she felt the world was unsafe. Her personality disorder is deeply rooted and was developed at a very young age. There wasn't really much her parents could do for her."

I felt badly for Marina, to say the very least. But I had a job to do and couldn't bring my emotions into it. "Okay," I said, "what can you tell me about Celia?"

"When Marina was 19, she moved in with Celia. Celia and she were best friends from the age of seven. I started treating Marina because of her issues with Celia. At that time, Celia was engaged and was going through the process of what happens when you find someone to marry and your interpersonal dynamics start to drastically change. You know, when two women are single and living together, you have a certain lifestyle, a certain dynamic. You're hanging out watching movies together, you're going to bars and restaurants together, you're staying up late nights talking and bonding.

Then, when one of the parties finds a relationship with the opposite sex, things change. You don't see your friend as much as you did before. You're not there when your friend wants to stay up late on a Friday night, drinking wine, eating chicken wings and binge-watching Netflix shows. One of the women is still making a standing Friday date in front of the television, but the other woman is entertaining an actual date that night. So, it's a time for change, and, for some, it's a time of profound loss. That is particularly true when the party left behind has a mental disorder."

I took notes while he spoke. I knew what he was saying was true - I knew enough women in my life to know how important their friends were, and how things change when one of them gets romantically involved with somebody.

"Things changed when Celia found a man to marry

named Frank Cerelli. She wasn't around as much, and then she told Marina that she would move in with Frank. When Celia started to stay away from the apartment at first, sometimes for days at a time, Marina came to see me. She was very distressed. She expressed dark fantasies about what she wanted to do to Celia and Frank."

"What kind of dark fantasies?" I asked.

"At first, it was simply that Marina wanted to end up in the hospital so that Celia would come back to her. She fantasized that she could get into a car accident that was serious enough that she would have to stay in the hospital for days or weeks, but not so serious that it would kill her. She explained that she thought Celia would come to her bedside and stay around her again. They'd watch movies on the hospital TV and play board games, and it would be just like old times."

That sounded innocent enough, I thought. I mean, it would obviously be twisted if somebody actually did something like that, but to think and fantasize about it? That didn't seem weird at all.

"What other kind of dark fantasies did she have?"

"That was it at first. That was the only dark fantasy she had expressed to me at that time. But she started to take other actions."

"Such as?"

"Stalking behavior. She would go by Frank's apartment every single day, just pop in unannounced, which was annoying for Celia, but harmless, I would imagine. But she also would sit in front of Frank's apartment and just watch for them to come out. She would break into Frank's home when he and Celia were out and would go through his personal things. She was looking for something that would make Celia want to dump him. She wanted to find any kind of incriminating evidence that maybe he was having an affair or was otherwise not loyal to Celia."

Dr. Alan hesitated and I thought something worse was coming. Much, much worse.

He continued on. "Eventually, she came around so much that Celia had to ask her to not come around anymore. Frank was getting annoyed and it was causing a strain on Celia's relationship with him. Marina told me she didn't take that well. She broke down crying and screaming and threatening Frank and Celia, and they got a restraining order against her."

Uh oh. Receiving a restraining order was hard for a normal person. I would imagine that somebody like Marina, who was mentally ill, would really have a hard time with that.

"Did Celia and Frank end up getting married?"

"No. Actually not. Frank was killed in a car accident. Celia thought Marina had something to do with it, so she moved away to the East Coast and Marina was never able to contact her. She disappeared, off the grid, no social pages, apparently changed her name."

"Why did Celia blame Marina for the accident?"

"She blamed Marina because, quite frankly, she was responsible for it. Nobody could ever prove anything, but the carpet on the driver side floorboard got stuck on top of Frank's gas pedal. It was never like that before. At least, that was what I understood from the police reports." He took a deep breath. "I'm telling you this because Marina expressly gave me permission to tell you. Otherwise, this would be confidential. But she came to see me yesterday and gave me explicit permission to discuss what she did to Frank."

"And did she actually do that to Frank?"

"She did, and Celia knew she did. Celia apparently saw

Insanity Defense

Marina do it. Or, rather, she saw Marina get into Frank's car and leave immediately. Marina tampered with Frank's car, and then she deliberately planted sexy text messages on Frank's phone. She knew Frank didn't check his text messages that often - he was a busy guy, and days would go by before he would even check them. Marina got a friend of hers to sext him and knew Celia would find the sext. She did, that caused a fight, and Frank left in a hurry. He apparently didn't notice the carpet issue because he stormed out of the house after being accused of something he didn't do. He ended up on the highway with his gas pedal stuck, so he started going 100 mph before he turned his car over in a ravine. He was killed instantly."

So Dr. Alan was telling me Marina was responsible for someone else's death. Lovely.

"So, she caused Frank's death, then?"

"She did." Dr. Alan nodded. "Again, she gave me explicit permission to tell you this. Because she gave this permission, I explained to her that confidentiality would be breached, which would mean she would potentially be held liable for Frank's death. But she was fine with this. She wanted you to know about this."

I would have to figure out what my responsibility was with this information. As her attorney, however, I knew I couldn't tell law enforcement about what she did. I had to have loyalty to my client.

"Okay, so what else can you tell me about her emotional issues?"

"First off, Marina is really two different people. I mean, I have not diagnosed her with Dissociative Identity Disorder, which is commonly known as multiple personality disorder. With Dissociative Identity Disorder, there are usually distinct personalities, and the classical way of thinking about it is that each personality has a different name, different behaviors, different tastes, different characteristics and each personality is separate and distinct. Marina does not have multiple personalities, at least not that I have been able to tell. But she has told me she has this part of her that is her shadow self. She calls her shadow self either Sarah or Malphas, which is the name of a demon in Christian theology. Whether the shadow self is referred to as Sarah or Malphas depends on the day. She wants her shadow to be Sarah. Because Sarah, in Marina's mind, is a good, kind, healthy person. But Marina thinks her shadow self is more like Malphas."

"I don't understand. Why is her shadow self called Malphas?"

"Because Malphas is the name of a Christian demon. According to Christian theology, Malphas is second in command to Satan, and is known for his destruction of his enemies. Marina has told me that she sometimes felt like a demon, one that only wants to destroy everything in its path."

"So this demon is –"

"Her shadow self. See, one of the classic signs of borderline personality disorder is that you don't have a stable sense of self. Sometimes you look in the mirror and you feel that the person looking back at you is somebody you really like, even love. You think the person in the mirror is a good, moral person. Other times, you look in the mirror and you see yourself as being horrible, evil. A devil. A demon. And it's that shadow self, the person who the borderline sees as being evil, who engages in the destructive behaviors. There are also emotional mood swings, from depression to being happy, to being despondent to being manic. Mood swings are things that flare up out of nowhere, but then they're gone. They can last a few minutes or a few hours."

I thought about what I saw back at Marina's house. How she went from happy and smiling, to hard and cold, to flirtatious, and then back to happy and smiling, all in just a matter of minutes.

The doctor went on. "Marina also is typical of patients with borderline personality disorder in that she has explosive anger that she cannot control. And she does have suicidal ideation. At least, that's what she tells me. She feels empty inside. Like there's nothing there. Void. She tells me that she often believes she doesn't have a soul."

All this wasn't sounding good. In fact, it was sounding as if there was a strong probability Marina killed her husband. The more I spoke with Dr. Alan, the more I started to believe an insanity plea was the way to go.

"Now tell me about the dissociation."

"Yes. Marina told me there have been times when she loses hours, even days. She doesn't really know why. But she has told me that, for instance, it'll be a Friday afternoon, and the last thing she remembered was going shopping at the mall the previous Monday. She would remember going to Bloomingdale's and the next thing she knows it's four days later and she's in her bed at home. She doesn't really know why that happens. As I said, I would suspect she had dissociative identity disorder, but I don't see any evidence of that. And dissociation is a fairly common symptom of borderline personality disorder. As with many patients with BPD, Marina's dissociation occurs when she's under a lot of stress. Because she's not always in touch with reality, she also feels suspicious of people and paranoid. She doesn't think people have the best motives for her. So you're going have a challenge with her as a client."

"Do you believe her? Do you believe she can't remember what happened when her husband was killed?"

"Yes. I do believe her. I know she was experiencing a great deal of stress at the time her husband was murdered. She's very open with me about things happening with her life. But, for some odd reason, she would not tell me what this particular stressor was. I tried to pry it out of her. I couldn't understand why she wouldn't tell me about it. After all, she told me about everything, including how she tampered with Frank's car causing his death. But, in this case, she told me that she could not explain exactly what was going on in her life. All I know is that, in the weeks leading up to her husband's death, she was frightened and also very angry."

Frightened, angry. And the weird thing is that Marina wasn't telling her shrink about exactly why she was frightened and angry. That was the strangest thing.

"Do you think she killed her husband?" I asked.

"It's impossible to say. I do believe that she told the truth when she says she doesn't remember that night. If that says anything at all."

I spoke with Dr. Alan for several more hours, and, after I talked with him, I knew what I had to do.

Chapter Twelve

THE HEARING on whether or not Marina was competent to stand trial was held that following Monday. That was after I spoke with her psychotherapist and I had my research all together. I got the response to my motion I filed asking the court to find my client not competent to stand trial, and I knew the prosecutor would argue that my client's amnesia from the night her husband died didn't preclude her standing trial for his murder. Jenna Powell was representing the state of California in this case. She was a longtime prosecutor with plenty of trial experience, and I knew she was anxious to eat me alive.

This hearing would give her the first shot at me, so I knew I had to bring my A game.

I had my case all together and knew that whether or not the judge would order Marina to stand trial was dependent on many factors. I would argue that, because Marina had no idea what happened the night her husband died, she couldn't assist me and couldn't testify on her own behalf about what happened that night. But another factor was whether or not the evidence could be extrinsically reconstructed, which meant I could still defend her by showing extrinsic evidence that she didn't do it.

That was really the rub. Truth be told, even though I made a motion about the competency issue, I also secretly wanted to lose this particular hearing. That was because I could try to reconstruct the evidence in this case. If there was any possibility that Marina had nothing to do with her husband's murder, I wanted to find that out. Because if she was deemed not competent to stand trial, she would possibly be committed to a mental institution for the rest of her life. That wouldn't be right if she didn't actually do it.

Yet, I also knew that if she did do it, it would be best if she didn't stand trial.

I made my arguments about the fact that Marina couldn't assist in her own defense, and Jenna made her arguments. She stated that, while there wasn't much case law in California about whether amnesia about a criminal act precluded the defendant being tried, she did cite one case, *People v. Amador*, a California Supreme Court case that stated that amnesia regarding a crime, in and of itself, did not automatically mean incompetence to stand trial.

"The California Supreme Court found that amnesia is not necessarily a reason to find a defendant incompetent because amnesia is easy to fake," Jenna told the court.

"But my client wasn't faking," I said. "She's been diagnosed with dissociation. I watched the interrogation between my client and the cops who brought her in and she was acting very different. Her face was blank, her words were rote, she didn't have emotions, and she wasn't answering the questions right. Her answers to the cops' questions were nonsensical. I could show your honor this interrogation record if that would help."

The judge took a deep breath. "That might be necessary, but let me listen to the rest of the arguments first."

"Another argument that the California Supreme Court made in *People v. Amador* was that a person with amnesia brought on by mental illness or trauma is no worse off than somebody who can't remember committing a crime because of excessive drinking or drug use, and sometimes people commit crimes while they're asleep and under the influence of Ambien or another powerful sedative," Jenna said. "It's against public policy to negate criminal responsibility because an individual was too drunk or drugged up to remember committing a crime, and, likewise, it is just as against public policy to negate criminal responsibility because an individual has amnesia. To negate criminal responsibility and allow defendants to avoid trial because they can't remember a crime would jeopardize the safety and security of law-abiding citizens."

"Your honor, I think we can all agree that amnesia brought on by mental illness is different than amnesia brought on by excessive drinking or drug-taking," I argued. "My client's memory loss was through no fault of her own. And even in the case of *People v. Amador*, the court stated the circumstances surrounding the amnesiac incident would be evaluated on a case by case basis. In this case, my client has been suffering from a long-standing mental illness and has had many dissociative states in the past, much like the state she was in at the time of the murder."

Judge Watts listened to both of our arguments and then nodded.

"Okay," she said after both of us presented our arguments. "I read my own case law on this matter, and it seems like the balance of the case law states that public policy would not be served if we decided to declare the amnesia was a catch-all reason for a finding of incompetency to stand trial. And, quite frankly, Mr. Collins, I don't know what I could even do with your client if I decided to declare her incompetent to stand trial. Because the problem is that people who are incompetent to stand trial are usually remanded to a mental institution, where they receive treatment, and, hopefully, they'll be declared competent to stand trial after the treatment.

In this case, because the incompetency stems from the fact that the client could not remember the crime in question, it would be impossible to ever bring her to the state where she's competent to stand trial. So it would be against public policy to state that she would never be able to stand trial for what the prosecutor alleged she did. So, because of that, I will go ahead and state your client is competent to stand trial. I will not have her evaluated by a psychotherapist for the competency issue. Now, I'm going to give a date for the formal arraignment for your client. If you would like to plead your client not guilty by reason of insanity, you can make this pleading then. I'm going to set that arraignment for Monday, July 5, three weeks from today."

I felt nervous. In three weeks I would have to decide whether or not to try for the insanity defense. Granted, I knew I could always withdraw that plea at some point in the future, if I found out that, in fact, Marina did not actually kill her husband.

So I would have to do as much of an investigation as I possibly could in the next three weeks to determine whether or not I wanted to go forward with the insanity plea.

Chapter Thirteen

THAT NIGHT, Regina finally agreed to have dinner with me. Well, that wasn't exactly true. She agreed to come over for dinner. Avery was fixing steaks on the grill and a baked potato with all the fixings, plus she had a bottle of Bordeaux chilling in the ice bucket on the patio.

Regina showed up that evening, looking as gorgeous as ever. She said she had some news for me about what was going on with my case. She then proceeded to tell me about Brock, and how strange she found him.

"I just don't know about that guy. He says he was involved with the two of them. And I guess he was. But why? And how? He would never explain it to me, but somehow I think he has some kind of information about the two of them he's just not divulging."

Avery poured the wine, and I took a sip of it while looking right at Regina.

"So, what are you thinking about that? Do you think that..."

"Well, I'd like to know it how he even knew her. And I

have a hunch he's on her side, not his. I just got that feeling from the way he talked."

"Is there anybody else you're going be talking to this week?" I asked Regina.

"Yes. As matter fact there is." She raised an eyebrow at me.

Avery looked at Regina with an expectant look on her face. "Go ahead, tell us who you're going to be talking to."

"Well, here's the thing. You know how Pegasus is involved in research. Trying to clone a human being and all that. Well, I spoke with a few people over a Pegasus, people who were not in management or anything like that, but are receptionists, secretaries, people like that who have their ears the ground and aren't too snobby to talk to me. They know the secrets of the organization. They've told me that Pegasus has already started working with some woman by the name of Helena Maxwell. Helena had a daughter whose name was Genevieve. Genevieve was only seven years old when she was killed in a car accident, and Helena cannot accept the fact that her daughter was killed. So she discovered the Pegasus company, found out about what they were doing and volunteered to be their first human test subject. She basically wants to bring Genevieve back to life. I know, I know, this is all science fiction, and I think it's bull crap. But Pegasus is getting close to cloning a human being, and, from what the secretaries tell me, this person would be re-created. In a lab."

"Okay. So, what are you thinking?"

"Here's what I'm thinking. I'm thinking that somebody got wind about what's happening with this Genevieve person. Somebody found out Pegasus had moved onto a human trial, and they killed Lawrence to stop him. That's what I think might've happened."

"And why would they want to frame my client?" I asked her. I admit, I was thinking along these lines myself. When a company is involved in a controversial line of research such as human cloning, there was bound to be some nut-case who gets pissed and tries to stop it.

"Who says they were framing your client? Listen, it's entirely possible that it was just bad luck that she had some kind of dissociative state at the time her husband died. Let's just say that somebody came upon what was happening, freaked out about it, went to his house, and shot him. And, all the while, your client was having a dissociative state, like she has from time to time. So the guy shoots Lawrence and leaves. In the meantime, your client is walking around the house, not really sure about what's going on, and the cops arrest her for the murder. She doesn't know if she did it or not. Anyhow, I need to find out if there's anybody who knew about what was going on with this Genevieve issue."

"That's an interesting way of looking at it. But what are you finding out with all the sexual partners?"

"Well I just talked to the one. And it turns out that he was not even one of the ones they were fooling around with. I still don't know what his deal is. I'd like to figure that one out myself. I'm going to keep talking to some of the people they were hooking up with on alt.com."

"Well, find out about the general situation and get back with me. Also try to find out if he had any other kind of enemies. He might have. You never know."

"Right, you never know. Don't worry, I'm doing my investigations. I'm going to try to figure something out. In the meantime, you just decide what you need to do with Marina."

Just then, the doorbell rang.

Avery went to answer it, and then, a second later, I

heard the familiar voice of Marina as she was coming to the door. "Hello, I hope I'm not interrupting anything."

I looked over at her. She was dressed in a very low cut blouse and tight jeans, which accentuated the curve of her perfect butt. The blouse clung to her rather full breasts. Like the other day, she wasn't wearing a lot of makeup, just some eyeshadow, some mascara, and some light lipstick, and her hair was natural - flowing around her shoulders in auburn ringlets. The way she looked at that moment, with her fresh face, she was even sexier then she was at her house.

Of course, I had to not think of her as sexy in any way, shape or form. If I did, I would get in trouble with her. There was no way I could ever get involved with a woman like this, not just because she's my client, but also because if I got involved with her, she would cause a lot of problems for me.

Her words from earlier echoed in my ears. *If you don't do what I say, you could use your license.* What did she mean by that? Did she mean that she would report me to the bar for something I didn't do? She was just the kind of person who would do some like that. I had to step lightly with her. To say the very least.

"Marina," I said to her. "Come in. We were just talking about your case."

She nodded. She looked over at everyone, and then at me. "Aidan, I'd like to talk to you alone. Please."

"Okay."

We went outside on the balcony, and I lit the fire ring. The coals came to life, lighting up the small balcony, and giving me the warmth that was welcomed, as it was unseasonably cool that evening. June gloom, which referred to the constant overcast days that San Diego experienced during

June, was in full force on that day, so the evening was very chilly.

"Okay, what did you need to say to me?"

She took a deep breath. "I just wanted to say that I don't want you to take this wrong way, but I don't think Regina should be on this case. I know the two of you are sleeping together. I've had too many experiences in the past where I had lawyers who were distracted by the people in their lives, either their wives, girlfriends, or investigators, and they don't tend to give my case their all."

I thought about how Regina had been treating me ever since the morning she woke up in bed next to me, and I knew that, unfortunately for me, Marina really had nothing to worry about. Regina had no interest in me, outside the professional realm.

"You're right. At least you were right the first time I saw you in the jail. Regina and I were sleeping together. But we're not anymore. We haven't been ever since that night. It was a one-night thing, not an on-going business. We were drinking that night, and that was that. So, in other words, you don't really have to worry about that."

She raised her eyebrows. "I don't think you understand. I just want you to be to be on my case. You and maybe your friend, that George guy, or whatever his name is. The one you chose to be your second chair. I don't mind him. I don't want a woman on your case. On this case." Then she cocked her head at me and looked at me coquettishly while her fingers lightly grazed my arm.

"Well, I don't think you have a say in this –"

"Oh, but I do. I do. I talked to James. I talked to James about this case, and he agrees with me. He agrees that he should not have a woman helping you. And he's the one paying the bills. He's the one paying you for this case. I know you need that job. I just have to go to James and say the word, and you'll not only be off my case, you'll be out of the firm completely."

I couldn't believe that what I was hearing from her. She was threatening me again. I was just going to have to talk to James and find out exactly why he was being so led around by the nose by this woman. Because it didn't make much sense to me.

"With all due respect –"

"What did the judge say today, about me being competent for trial?"

"Just what I thought she would say. She said that case law was clear that just because you can't remember a crime doesn't mean you're incompetent for trial and she was also concerned that if she said that you weren't competent to stand trial now that you could never stand trial. She didn't know what to do with you. Because it's not like you could be brought back to competency in this case. Obviously."

Marina smiled a little bit and nodded. "You see. I told you."

"No, I don't really see what you're saying. Maybe I just don't want to see what you're saying." I was getting irritated with her. I didn't know why, but I just knew she was trying to mess with me somehow.

Just then, she closed her eyes. When she opened them again and looked at me, just like earlier that day, her face changed. Changed from the soft, feminine, pretty face to one that was hard, mean, ugly.

She stood up and punched me hard in the face. Then she leaned close to me, and I shoved her off me. She leaned closer me again, and she said something to me, in a voice that sounded like it was coming from another dimension. It was guttural, low, growling. "I know you were trying to say that you were not going to do the things I asked you to do, but you're going to. You're going to. I don't want Regina on this case... she's not going to be on this case, and you're not going to defy me. If you do, you'll see what happens."

At that, she went into the condo, and stormed out the door.

"What's going on out here?" Regina said.

"You tell me. All I know is I'm going to have to talk to James tomorrow and I'm going to have to get off this case. I can't handle this woman. She's just too volatile. And she doesn't want you on the case. She doesn't want any woman on the case."

Chapter Fourteen

I WENT to see James the next day, to tell him he needed to reassign Marina's case to somebody else.

"I'm afraid I can't do that," James said to me.

"What do you mean, you can't do that?" I asked him.

"Listen, here's the thing." He went to the door of this office and shut it. "Now listen, you can't say a word of this to anybody. You can't breathe a word. If you do, I'll just deny everything, and you'll be out of a job. I can fire you for any reason. Or no reason at all. Just remember that."

I closed my eyes as I thought about whether or not I really wanted to work at this place. But then again, jobs were not exactly easy to come by. I wasn't top of my class, unlike my sister. I didn't graduate from Harvard Law like she did - I graduated from the University of San Diego. This was a good job. I was lucky to get it. I knew far too many of my law school chums were currently working at Starbucks, trying to pay off their student loans on an $18 an hour salary. Making cappuccinos for the same yuppies who were at the law firms where they were coveting a position.

No, I needed this job. If I didn't want to become a complete and total wipeout in my life, I needed this job.

"Okay, go on."

"This firm is not exactly, shall we say, solvent," he continued on in a low voice. "We have a lot of expenses here. And I just found out the managing partner, Bart, he left before you got here, was embezzling from the company. Millions of dollars. He went to prison for it last month and has been ordered to pay restitution to the firm, but he doesn't have the money anymore. He gambled it all away at the casinos, but he also lost a lot of it in the stock market. Turns out he was not a very good investor. Not very smart in that way. And he not only took a lot of wealth out of this company, but he also managed to get us in trouble with the IRS. He was the one who was managing the taxes. And apparently the auditing firm was incompetent. To say the very least. So now, this firm owes millions of dollars to the IRS as well.

So, what I'm trying to tell you is that if we want to stay afloat, we need Marina's business. We need her millions. We're billing her at $1000 an hour for your services. Hopefully by the end of this, we will have billed her $4 million or more. Now that's not going to necessarily going to make a dent in what Bart did to us, but it will certainly go a long ways towards making sure that we can buy some time until the IRS comes and shuts us down. So, basically, if she says jump, we say how high. And that's that."

That was still the strangest thing to me. Why did she want me so badly that she would pay a thousand dollars an hour for my services? Granted, I was only getting paid my usual associate salary, $50,000 a year, but she was paying this firm a lot of money. Why?

"Okay, I see. So I can't get off of her case. Why don't you try to assign it to somebody else in the firm?"

"I won't, because she wants you. And that's all there is to it." He put his hands up as if to say *I don't know what her deal is either.* "So, I'm very sorry, but you have to do what she says. You cannot withdraw from her case. If she doesn't want Regina on the case, then she doesn't want Regina on the case. It looks like you're going to have to do your own investigations. I know you can do it. And, if you want, of course, George will help you. He's your second chair, use him."

"You don't understand. She's not listening to me. She keeps telling me that she doesn't want me to plead her not guilty by reason of insanity, and that's exactly what I'm going to try to do." Well, that wasn't exactly true. Sometimes she was just fine with me pleading her NGRI. Other times, she hit me and screamed at me like a banshee when I told her my plans for her case. Which was another reason why I desperately needed to withdraw.

"Listen, you have to go with what she wants," James said. "Now, I agree, she probably isn't in her right mind. I don't dispute that at all. I've met her, and while she is incredibly physically beautiful, to say the very least, she isn't right. And that's all I can really say about it. But if she says she doesn't want an insanity plea, then don't do it. That's all I can say."

"But isn't that malpractice?" I asked. "If I truly think she didn't have the *mens rea* to have killed her husband that night, and she did in fact kill her husband, and the jury finds her guilty, and not clinically insane according to the M'Naghten rule, then what am I even doing in the practice of law? If she belongs in a mental institution for the rest of her life, not prison, then it's my job to make sure a mental institution is where she ends up."

"I don't know what to tell you. All I can say is that you need to tread lightly with this one. We need her money. And, as I said, she wants only you. I asked her if she'll take another attorney from this firm. Because, as I told her, you don't know what you're doing. But she wants you. And that's that. So whatever she wants, you have to give it to her. End of story."

I was frustrated. I felt trapped, like I would be heading down the path I didn't want to go down. Was she setting me up? Was she going to sue me for malpractice after everything was said and done? Was she going to appeal the case on the basis of ineffective assistance of counsel? Was I going to be humiliated after all of this?

Maybe that was her deal all along. Maybe she wanted to humiliate me. Maybe she hated me. Maybe she wanted me to stew in my own juices.

I didn't really know. All I knew was that I was stuck with this case. I would have to follow her lead, against my better judgment.

And there was nothing I could do about it.

Chapter Fifteen

MARINA

MARINA SAT IN HER MANSION, putting powder on her elbows and on her face. She got closer to the mirror. It was a magnifying mirror, one that showed all of her tiny flaws. Most of the time when she looked in that mirror, she loved what she saw. She knew she was gorgeous. She knew she had beautiful creamy skin, clear blue eyes, a very symmetrical, oval face, cheekbones that could cut glass, and a very light and delicate nose. She knew her body was perfect. Her waist was tiny, her breasts were small but perky, her butt was rounded and her legs firm.

But other times she looked in the mirror and saw nothing but a mass of wrinkles. She would see a monster staring at her, one with a gaping maw of teeth that looked like it could come out of the mirror and eat her alive. When she was in the state where she would see the hag in the mirror, she tried not to look at herself.

She wished she could get herself under control, but she just couldn't. What her husband did to her was unforgivable. Absolutely unforgivable.

But what she was doing to Aidan was just as unforgivable. He didn't deserve her as a client. And in certain states of mind, she knew it. He was just an innocent kid. A newbie, a greenie, a guy just out of law school and trying to do the best he could on her case, and she was not making it easy for him.

But it had to be him. That's all she knew. It had to be him because she really didn't care if she lived or died.

When she was a young girl, growing up in the orphanage in Russia, she learned how to take the abuse given to her. She learned that she could leave her body at any given time. She practiced it for many years. When the men would be doing to her what they did to her, when she was only three years old, and four years old, and five years old, and six years old, and seven years old, she learned to just leave. Go someplace else. She would do what her psychotherapist said was disassociate. And, over the years, it saved her. Whenever she had stressful periods in her life, she would leave. Go someplace else.

All she could think about when she was over in Russia, in that orphanage, was that she desperately wanted somebody to save her. And she always thought she had a sister somewhere. It was just something in her brain. She almost could remember when she was a very little girl, less than one-year-old, before her parents died in an accident. Actually, it wasn't necessarily an accident, they were disappeared by the Russian government. They were both dissidents. At least that's what she was told about her parents when she got to be an adult. But she could almost remember there was somebody who was with her when she was a baby. The memory was hazy, obviously, because she was extremely young. But she remembered being with somebody, somebody laying next to her in her crib.

And she carried that vague memory with her throughout her days of hell in the orphanage.

Of course, she always thought she was imagining it. Of course she didn't have a sister. If she did have a sister, where was she all this time? It didn't make any sense. After all, if she had a sister, her sister would have been brought with her to the orphanage, and she wasn't. So, Marina just assumed this sister of hers was just a figment of her imagination.

She took a deep breath, and took one last look in the mirror. She was going out that night. Out to dinner. And she couldn't be late.

She wondered, as she looked at herself in the mirror, if she was doing the right thing. If everything went well, she would end up in an orange jumpsuit jumpsuit for real. Not that she minded that. It wasn't exactly going to be the best thing in the entire world for her, to say the very least. But she already had a plan. She would just go to the prison and make sure that she took her meds. Her doctor had prescribed meds for bipolar disorder, which she didn't really have, but it was never ruled out, since borderline personality disorder is so similar to bipolar in so many ways. So she convinced the psychiatrist to give her those meds.

The plan was to take those meds, one by one, and store them in her cheeks. Sooner or later, she would accumulate enough of those pills that she could take them all at once and put herself out of her misery. It's what she wanted to do anyways. It's what she had always wanted to do.

And if that happened, she could save her.

She could save the one who did it for real.

Chapter Sixteen

THE NEXT DAY, it was time to talk to Regina about her not being allowed to investigate Marina's case anymore. I still was unclear on exactly why Regina couldn't do this investigation for me. All I knew was that James told me Regina couldn't be on the case because Marina didn't want her there.

I went to meet with Regina at one of our favorite restaurants - In and Out. People who lived east of the Rockies didn't know what they were missing with these hamburgers. As usual, there was a line out the door for this place.

I got my usual, the double-double cheeseburger and a large fry. Regina got the same. I looked at her, wondering where she put all that food, but then again, she could say the same thing about me. I was 6'2" and 170 lbs myself. I knew the reason I could eat like this was because I was very active. I was training for a triathlon. Every morning I rode my bike before work, or ran along the beach, or swam in the ocean.

Still, the junk food I got at In and Out, the double

double cheeseburger and the french fries, wasn't something I could get all the time. I didn't like the way that crap made me feel, but it was delicious, that was for sure.

Regina seemed to already know what I was going to talk to her about. "You're firing me, aren't you?" she asked.

I took a deep breath. "Yes. I'm sorry. I have to. For some odd reason, Marina just doesn't want you on the case."

"You're going to regret this. So who's going to be doing the investigations?"

"I am."

Regina snorted. "You are?" Her eyes narrowed as she sat across from me. "No offense, but does this woman have a death wish? I mean, she's insisting on you taking her case, even though you don't know what you're doing. Then she's insisting on you not having an investigator. There's something that just isn't right about all of this. It doesn't pass the smell test. I think I need to find out exactly what it is."

"I wish you could. I need you on this case. I don't know what I'm doing."

Regina got quiet as she ate her burger and fries, which was highly unusual for her. "Well," she finally said, "I guess what's done is done. So what's next in the case?"

"I was unable to have her declared incompetent to stand trial, and she's tying my hands as to whether or not she wants me to put in an insanity plea. She doesn't want me to do that."

"Then you have to. She doesn't remember what happened the night of the murder. Right? And now that you don't have an investigator, you probably won't be able to find out if that chick did it or not, so you might as well plead her insane."

"That's right, she doesn't remember the night of the murder." I wanted to tell Regina about what Dr. Alan had told me about Marina. About how Marina was responsible for the death of somebody. Not just somebody, but the husband of her best friend. I wanted to tell Regina about how Marina dissociated. She had entire days she lost. Days where she had no idea what happened. But I knew this was all confidential information, so I couldn't tell Regina.

I couldn't say a word to her.

Regina sighed. I could tell she was annoyed. She tapped her fingers on the table, and then looked away. "You know Aidan, I'm just so surprised that you didn't fight for me. And I really hate the fact that I've been taken off this case before it's finished. Hell, I only got to talk to that one person, and I don't think he was any help at all."

"Brock, right?"

"Yeah. It was the weirdest thing, that guy. I wanted to dig into it and see if I can figure out exactly who he was. And I think he had information that would've led me to who I really needed to talk to. I mean-"

I had to interrupt her, because I was getting a phone call. It was Marina's number, so I knew I had to take it.

"Hello, honey," Marina's voice dripped with sweetness. I knew I was talking to her, not Malphus, the demon that Dr. Alan had told me about.

"Hi Marina, what's up?" I asked her.

"Listen, I want you to do what you need to do. In my case. If you think it's best that you make a plea of not guilty by reason of insanity, try that."

I was suspicious, to say the least, and wanted to record this conversation, because I just knew she would turn 180 degrees again on this situation and come back to bite me.

So, I turned on my phone recorder. "Okay, I'll see what I can do."

"Well, what does that mean?"

"That means I'll make a plea, but I'm going to try to convince the judge to let me withdraw that plea at any time. This is an unusual case, but not really. This isn't the first time somebody has tried a case where he's not quite sure if the person did it or not. So, if things come to light that shows you didn't actually do it, and then –"

"No. I don't want you to do that. I don't want you to try to talk to the judge about withdrawing the plea at any time. I want you to make sure you keep the insanity plea. Don't try to find anybody else who might've done this. Do you hear what I'm saying? My doctor will tell the court that I dissociated the night my husband was found, and that I did it."

"Marina, the only reason you were arrested for killing your husband is because you were in the house at the time he was found." Well, that and the fact that there were apparently witnesses who will testify about how cruel Marina was to her husband, but that was besides the point. "They don't know where the gun is, so there's no way the prosecutor can trace your fingerprints on the murder weapon. As far as I know, you don't really have a motive to have killed him. You don't remember. I'm just not convinced that you were responsible for him dying."

"Okay, okay. Listen. I've been lying to you all along. I don't have any memory loss. I know exactly what I did."

I looked over at Regina. "I'm so sorry, but I'm going to have to cut this lunch short. I think I'm going to have to meet with my client and talk to her about this. Because all of a sudden, she's singing a different tune."

"Suit yourself," Regina said. "I'm done anyway. Although I would like to get a chocolate milkshake."

"Marina, we need to talk," I said to Marina over the phone. "We need to meet. Where would you like to meet?"

"You can come to my house, but I really don't want you to. I just want you to listen to me. In fact, I want you to plead me guilty."

This wasn't right. Obviously. She was suddenly changing her mind about everything.

"Marina, I can't do that."

"You will do that." Her voice was hard, cold, commanding.

"Just sit tight. I'll be there in about a half-hour."

I hung up the phone. "That was my client. Obviously. She's freaking out, for some reason."

"Why? What's she saying?"

"She says she wants me to plead her guilty. But I can't do that. She has to make a factual basis to the court, and that means she's going to have to give all the facts about what happened that night. But, considering the fact that when they brought in for questioning, she was in a dissociative state, and was only brought out of it the day after the murder, she can't possibly make a factual basis."

"The judge won't accept a guilty plea from her?" Regina asked.

"No. Not under these circumstances. I suppose the judge might be able to accept a guilty plea from her if I put her under hypnosis and I brought back the memories of that night. But, that's not exactly scientifically sound. I don't believe it myself. She already told the cops that she had no memory and she was already diagnosed by a doctor as having been in a dissociative state at the time of the murder. I can't see her getting on the stand and making a factual basis for the guilty plea, and the judge actually accepting it. So, we're probably going to have to go forward with this trial, come hell or high water."

Regina went up and got a chocolate shake, and I went

up and did the same. We left the restaurant, both of us dipping our spoons into the cold concoction.

Regina took me to my office, and dropped me off, because that was where my car was.

I got in my car and drove off.

Chapter Seventeen

"WHAT DO YOU MEAN, you can't plead me guilty?" Marina asked me. She was shaking all over, pacing the floor. She looked like a caged animal. I looked in her eyes, and it looked like she was about ready to attack me again. Of course, if she did attack me again, I would be ready for it. The previous two times she attacked me, I wasn't ready for her, and I was sucker punched every time. This time, I would be able to defend myself.

"I mean that I can't plead you guilty. You told the cops that you had no memory of the night your husband died. You've told me, over and over, that you have no memory of the night your husband died. You simply cannot tell the court that you killed this man. If I let you do that, I'll be suborning perjury. If you want to plead guilty, you need to tell the court that you did it, and you can't do that. The judge won't accept your plea."

"But I did do it. I remember now. I remember shooting him in the face three times. I was furious with him that day. He was cheating on me with a woman I didn't like, and you know I'm capable of killing somebody. I know you talked to my doctor. I told Dr. Alan that he could tell you anything at all. That was the reason why Dr. Alan told you about my friend Celia and what I did to her husband. I did that to him. So you know I'm incapable of doing absolutely anything."

"Listen, Marina, I think we need to go ahead with the original plan to say you were not guilty by reason of insanity," I said.

"No. I don't want take any chances here. I –"

"What do you mean, you don't want take any chances?"

She swallowed hard. "I just mean that I don't want to take any chances that…"

"That, what?"

"I just want to pay for what I did. That's all. I deserve to be punished. I'm a terrible person. I did terrible things. Not just to my husband, but to a lot of other people. I'm a dangerous person. I need to be locked up."

"Marina where is this coming from?" I kind of knew that answer to that question. Dr. Alan told me she had an unstable sense of herself - she sometimes thought that she was great and other times she thought she was worthless trash.

"I told you, I killed that guy Frank. I was responsible for him dying. I was never punished for that. I mean, Celia moved away and never spoke to me again, so I guess I was punished that way. She knew what I did, but she could never prove it. That was why nothing ever happened to me for that."

I sighed and steepled my hands. "Marina, that's not how it works. You got away with murder once before. You can't go to prison for something you didn't do, just because you did something else in the past. I know that probably doesn't seem like it's justice to you, or to a lot of people, but that's how it is. You got away with killing him. Now, you don't know if you killed your husband or not. That's legit. You're not going to prison if you didn't actually kill him."

She studied me and, while she did, she put her hand up to her chest and put her fingers between her breasts and down to her stomach. Then she touched my hand, and, in spite of myself, I felt a tingle go up and down my arm. I was feeling things I didn't really want to feel. Maybe I was just amped up because of my frustration with Regina.

"Do you know why I did what I did to Frank?" she asked.

"Yeah. Dr. Alan told me that you were jealous of him, because he took your best friend away."

She shook her head. "No, that's not why I did it. I did it because he wasn't a good person. I tried to tell Celia about it. I tried to explain to her about the night he was alone with me. I was over at their house. I came over unannounced, as I always did. I was always coming around, just popping in out of nowhere. Celia was getting tired of me coming over out of the blue."

I thought about what Dr. Alan told me, and I knew Marina was right about that. Her friend definitely was getting tired of Marina coming over unannounced, to the point that Celia had taken out a restraining order against her.

"Well, on that day, I was there at the house. Celia wasn't there. I forget where he said she was, maybe at the store. Usually, I would just leave and come back, but on that day, Frank told me I could stay and wait for her to come home. I thought he was being nice for once in his life. So I took a seat on the couch."

She got up from where she was sitting, and then started

pacing the floor again. "Five minutes after I got there, Frank attacked me. He told me he lied to me. Celia was not coming home anytime soon. In fact, she was gone for the evening. She was seeing some friends. That hurt me bad. She had other friends she was seeing. She would never see me willingly. Never return my phone calls. This was my best friend. We lived together for three years. We grew up together. She was my first friend when I came to America - we met in the second grade. I was very behind in my studies, didn't know much English, felt very afraid and out of place. She saw I was lost and alone and she became my friend. My only friend. And here she was, hanging out with friends, while not willingly hanging out with me anymore. That was all I could think about. That was all I was thinking about as Frank took off his jeans, and then ripped off my dress."

I didn't know if she was telling me the truth or not. For that matter, maybe she was lying to her therapist in the first place. Maybe she was lying about killing Frank. Maybe there is never a Celia. She was the kind of person who would make up stories like that just to get a reaction from somebody.

I wished I had Regina's ability to read when somebody is lying. I didn't quite have that same ability, and I had never experienced being around somebody who was as gifted of a liar is this woman was. Not to mention the fact that she was, to say the very least, changeable.

Still, I let her go on.

"He raped me. He raped me right there on that couch. And I never told my friend about it. I didn't tell her because I didn't want her to know what kind of person she would be married to. She never would have listened to me anyways. Nobody ever does in situations like that. You know, when you're in love with somebody, you intend to marry them, and he's your entire world, and somebody tries to tell you something that makes you doubt that person's love for you. You're going to just explain it away. You're going to say the person is mistaken. You're going to say the person is lying. I just didn't want him to come between us. I loved her. Not in that way, but as a best friend. I can honestly say that I don't think I would have survived my childhood if not for her. So, I just didn't want anything to come between the two of us.

So that night, after I left their house, I was watching the news. I saw a story about a couple who had an accident in a car. I think it was a Toyota. It was defective, because the gas pedal got stuck underneath the carpet. Anyhow, this couple died because the gas pedal was stuck. And I knew that I would have to do that to him. I arranged everything. I needed them to get into a huge fight, so it would make him less likely to notice the gas pedal was underneath the car carpet. I tampered with the car. He crashed, just like I knew he would. And that's what happened."

I was just skeptical that the story was even true. "What did you say his name was again?"

"Frank Tobias."

"I hope you don't mind, I don't want to offend you, but maybe I do. But I'm going to Google that."

She shrugged. "Go ahead. You don't believe what I'm saying, go ahead and check it. You'll see."

I did check it. I Googled the name Frank Tobias, and the words car accident. Several stories immediately came up about the accident. According to these stories, he died because his gas pedal was stuck underneath his car carpet, and he ended up going 100 mph on the highway and rolled his car into a ravine. He was killed instantly.

But could I trust her? Maybe Marina saw this article

and used it to concoct a story about her killing this guy. Maybe she never even knew him at all. I didn't trust her any further than I could throw her.

"Why did you tell me this?" I asked her.

"Because I want you to know I'm capable of anything."

I shook my head. "I'm sorry, I just don't believe this story. I know your therapist said that's what happened, but that's because you told him this story. I don't believe you even knew this guy Frank Tobias, let alone killed him."

Maybe it way was the way she was telling me this story so nonchalantly that I just didn't believe her. She told the story about him raping her the way she would tell me about the cake she was making for dessert that evening. Two cups of sugar, two cups of flour, butter, pinch of salt. Oh and I murdered somebody after he raped me. That was the way she told the story. It was almost like it was an afterthought.

"You don't believe my story. That's okay, you soon will. You'll soon believe that and a whole lot more."

Somehow, when she said that, it sounded like a threat.

Chapter Eighteen

THE NEXT DAY, I decided that I would start my investigation at the Pegasus company. There was just something about the whole cloning thing that was sticking in my craw. I had read up about the cloning issue with regards to Pegasus and discovered that the company was conducting twin studies. For some odd reason, the whole twin studies was something that stood out to me, so I decided to make an appointment with the person in charge of that particular department for Pegasus.

Dr. Weber was considered to be one of the leading researchers on genetic influences and how they affect traits, disorders and phenotypes.

He agreed to meet with me over lunch, explaining to me that lunchtime was the only time he had to meet with people, because he was busy the rest of the day. He also told me that he found it important to speak with me, which was encouraging.

We made an arrangement to meet at a seafood restaurant on the water next to Seaport Village. Seaport Village was an area in San Diego that was bordering the San Diego Bay. It was a consortium of tiny mom and pop shops and restaurants. On the weekends, you'd find everything from psychics giving tarot readings to young Mexican women selling homemade jewelry. One guy was famous for balancing twenty stones, one on top of the other.

The restaurant was kind of an old-school seafood restaurant with a wooden facade, like you might see in Maine, and it had a large dining room that looked out onto the water.

I met Dr. Weber there. He was already waiting for me in the enclosed dying room. Dr. Weber was about 50 years old, with salt-and-pepper hair at the temples and a weathered face.

He stood up and shook my hand as I sat down, and I felt like an absolute kid next to him. I didn't know why I felt that way, except that he kind of reminded me of my dad.

"I'm really glad you wanted to meet with me." He put his napkin in his lap as I sat down. He had a bottle of wine in front of him, and he poured me a glass. "I just had a feeling you were going to want to find out about this research and what we're doing. When Lawrence was murdered, I knew my department would be the first place people would start looking. I figured it was probably good to get on top of it."

His eagerness to talk to me was just a little bit unsettling. I got that he wanted to get ahead of it. But what exactly was he getting ahead of?

"I'm really glad you wanted to meet with me as well." I took a sip of the wine. It was something smooth, dry. Some kind of Chablis or Chardonnay. I wasn't really sure, because I didn't know my wines all that well. All that I knew that it was quite tasty, fruity and cool. And it was welcome, considering it was a hot day outside.

Looking out the window, I realized how much I really wanted to be in my wetsuit and riding the waves, not talking to this guy in this restaurant. But it was what it was.

"So what kind of information do you want from me?" he asked.

"I just wanted to know what exactly you were doing, as far as with your twin studies."

"Well, it's just like it says. I've been conducting studies on identical and fraternal twins. Mostly identical twins, however. This is been going on for quite a long time. We hardly are at the forefront of this research. We've been studying how identical twins that have 100% of the same gene are different from one another, and why they're different. We specifically study twins because we want to see what the impact is on nature versus nurture."

"I see. And what is the purpose of this twin studies for your company?" I asked.

"It has to do with our cloning research. I'm sure you're aware that we are on the forefront of that particular field. There is a race to see who can be the first to clone a human being. It's much like the space race from the 1960s. I understand that a lot of people have a lot of problems with the concept of cloning. The bioethics of it and all of that. But you have to understand that there are certain reasons why parents might want to have their child cloned. And I can assure you that it has nothing to do with the desire to have an extra child that would be able to donate organs to the first child. That, of course, would be murder, and it is not something that we would ever condone."

"Tell me about the cloning procedures your company is

involved with," I said to him. "And then tell me how your twin studies relates to it."

He nodded and took a sip of his wine. "Well, there are two kinds of human cloning. Therapeutic cloning and reproductive cloning. Therapeutic cloning is very beneficial for society. It's something that's relatively noncontroversial. It's responsible for many breakthroughs."

"Tell me what therapeutic cloning is, exactly."

"It's basically cloning cells, genes and tissues, and this cloning cannot lead to another human being," he said. "It's what's called a somatic cell nuclear transfer. We take the nucleus of an egg and replace it with the nucleus of somatic cells, such as skin cells, and then the cell divides. Because the egg is never fertilized, the genetic material is identical to the genetic material extracted from the skin. This can create stem cells which are a genetic match for the patient. These stem cells can be used to treat brain diseases such as Parkinson's disease or ALS, and also other diseases such as diabetes."

"Okay, that sounds very good. Can you give me some examples as to how this kind of cloning can help somebody?"

"Sure. Let's just take a man who has had a heart attack. Let's just say this man is not eligible for a heart transplant. The heart attack has weakened his heart so much that it has destroyed two-thirds of his heart. He would not be able to return to his active life."

"Okay. Go on."

I took some of the bread out of the basket, put some butter on it, and popped a small bit into my mouth. I waited for him to explain to me more about the whole therapeutic cloning scenario. I had admit, this was fascinating for me.

"Well, therapeutic cloning can regenerate new heart

muscle. See, what happens is that the scientist can take a small sample of the skin cells and take the genetic material from the cell and inject it into a donated human egg. That egg will have the chromosomes taken out of it, and the egg is altered with his DNA from his skin cells. This creates stem cells that can become heart muscle cells or brain cells or any other kind of cells that are a perfect genetic match for the patient. And then the cells can be injected into the heart, to replace the cells that were lost during a heart attack."

"And this is what your company has been focused on?"

"Yes. We have been focused on therapeutic cloning, and also making embryonic stem cells using this same method. As you know, embryonic stem cells are a controversial subject in this country, because there's a pro-life contingent who object to embryonic stem cells being studied and used for any kind of research. So, because therapeutic cloning can create these embryonic stem cells, we can get around the whole controversy about people believing that obtaining embryonic stem cells is illegal. In other words, therapeutic cloning really adds a great deal to the advancement of our knowledge of the human body, and our ability to treat many diseases."

"I have studied a little bit about the whole therapeutic cloning issue, before I came to see you, but I understand that the Pegasus company is not just involved with therapeutic cloning. You're also involved with reproductive cloning. Isn't that right?" I asked.

"Yes, of course. I suppose that's the reason why you wanted to talk to me. Because that obviously is a more controversial area. People get really, for lack of a better word, weirded out by the whole concept of reproductive cloning. But, really, it's not necessarily that controversial. Or it shouldn't be. It's just another method of creating a new life."

"What, in your view, are the advantages of having a cloned child, as opposed to, maybe, having a child naturally or going through in vitro fertilization or another method to have a child?"

"Good question. There are certain advantages that human cloning might have over your standard in vitro fertilization. For instance, if you have a child through standard in vitro fertilization, there's always a chance that the child will have some kind of a genetic malady. Such as, for instance, Down's Syndrome or Huntington's Disease, or any number of diseases that are caused by some kind of a defective gene. With human cloning, if it is perfected, the child won't be born with such maladies, because the child will be born with the genetic code of the donor. So that's one obvious upside to human cloning as opposed to standard *in vitro* fertilization."

As he spoke, I started thinking about the concept of eugenics, and about the Nazis. They would love this guy.

"Another advantage to human cloning, as opposed to *in vitro* fertilization, is, and I know this is controversial, but there are some parents who sincerely want to clone their child. Especially a child that has died. They desperately want to bring that child back, and if you actually bring that child back through cloning, it will be as if the child never died."

"So that's where the twin studies come into play, right?"

"Right. We obviously are interested in the nature versus nurture controversy, and how nurturing can affect the child's upbringing, a child's disposition, and so forth. We want to be able to explain to parents who would use our services in the future, when our cloning technique is perfected, exactly what they would be looking at as far as their deceased child coming back into their lives. We want to be able to tell them, with some degree of certainty, how much the new child will be like the previous child. In order to do that, we need to know much more about how much the role of nurturing plays on that child."

"Are you at all aware that what you're doing smacks of eugenics?" I asked him.

He sat back in his chair, and steepled his hands. I could tell he was used to being asked this very question, and he had a ready answer.

"No. Not at all. You see, there's a societal cost to genetic disorders. A very high societal cost. Individuals who have genetic disorders not only cost the healthcare system a lot of money, but they also are, for lack of a better word, a drag on our economy. An individual with Down's Syndrome can't contribute much, if at all, to society, over the course of his or her life. That child is never going to be able to cure cancer, or find or produce the latest software miracle. Most likely, the child will end up being institutionalized for the rest of his or her life, at the taxpayers' expense. Of course, that's not always the case, because oftentimes parents want to care for the child on their own. But that child will also incur expenses, societal expenses, because the parents would be entitled to collect disability payments for him or her. The child will use up an inordinate amount of medical resources, which makes everybody's health care costs rise. Everybody pays.

And if an individual has some other disease that is caused by a defective gene, such as Type 1 Diabetes, Huntington's Disease or Sickle Cell Anemia, that person is going to cost the health care system millions of dollars over the course of his or her life. Insulin is extremely expensive, and that's something that will cost every person who in the insurance pool. If your insurance costs are sky high, the reason for that is because there are so many sick people in the world. When insurance companies have to pay millions of dollars for the treatment of one person, they have to pass those costs along to everyone else. A lot of the sicknesses that we are experiencing in this world can be eliminated through the proper application of genetic therapy, which would include the possibility of human cloning."

"So, perhaps you'd like to create a master race? Maybe you'd like for society to just be composed of people who can give back and the people who are less fortunate, who don't have the ability to give back to society, through no fault of their own, should be eliminated?"

"You make it sound as if I'm a monster. I'm not. Listen, we have a lot of problems in this country. In this world. A lot of people are miserable, for various reasons. Do you think an individual who is dying of ALS, which is, I can assure you, a most horrible death, is happy? Would you like to lose the ability to speak, all of your cognitive facilities, the ability to walk, the ability to bathe yourself, while knowing you're going to die anyway? Do you believe that the parent of a Down's Syndrome child is happy? I know, a lot of them say they are, but it has to wear on them. Caring for a profoundly disabled child, day after day, is taxing, stressful. Some of the genetic diseases are monstrous. They are diseases I wouldn't wish upon anybody in this world. If we could avoid them, why wouldn't we?"

I could tell he was getting defensive. And why shouldn't he? I was asking him sharp questions, and he probably was not expecting that I would be asking these kinds of questions of him.

"So, are you also going to, maybe, only take genetically

superior people for your client experiments? I mean, if an individual came to you, and this person happened to be of low intellect, or had some other kind of disability, would you take that person on as a potential client? Would you want to clone that person?"

The doctor was silent, which spoke volumes. I could tell he was thinking in his mind that no, we would only take people who are genetically superior. People who are of sound intellect with no kind of defects.

He really was trying to build a master race.

"Society will thank me, and our company, over the years. In 50 years, if human cloning becomes a practice that is accepted, and utilized, I would think our society will be much better off for it. Listen, nobody wants their child to have a genetic disorder. Nobody. If there's a way to avoid that, why wouldn't you? Why wouldn't you want to have a child that you can be assured is free of any kind of genetic disorder? A child who for sure will not have disabilities, who is physically able to contribute to society as much is he or she possibly can. Let's face it, if you have a child, either through the normal way or through *in vitro* fertilization, it's a crap shoot. Anything can happen with that child. Anything can affect the child's genetic code and cause him or her to be something less-than."

I raised an eyebrow. "Something less than what?"

"Something less than fully human."

I sat back in my chair and crossed my arms in front of me. I was starting to wonder if this guy was defective himself. Mentally defective. He certainly was open with what his company was trying to do, and proud of it. Who says things like *a child with a disability is less than human* in front of someone that he or she just met?

I represented people like him in the mental institutions I

worked at. They were called sociopaths. Not that this guy necessarily was a sociopath, because I didn't know if he had a conscience. However, he certainly had a warped view of the world.

The guy went on. "Look at all the diseases caused by genetics. Cystic fibrosis, which is a hideous disease that damages the lungs and the digestive system. You have to constantly break up the fibroids in your lungs and people who suffer from that disease have infections throughout most of their lives. CF affects every organ in the body, like the pancreas, because it prevents the release of digestive enzymes and it affects the liver because it blocks the bile ducts, which causes liver disease. Children with CF have stunted growth and, as with all major genetic diseases, they incur a lot of medical bills. Sickle-cell anemia causes a lot of pain and infections, along with delayed growth and vision problems. Again, they're a tax on our medical system. The list goes on. I don't know about you, but I would like to live in a world where there's less suffering. One of the ways of doing that is to make sure that only the best genetics are passed on from one person to another."

I decided to just go ahead and let him talk. I was having a feeling that there was something off about this guy.

He seemed to be capable of murdering somebody. In fact, I was surprised he wasn't telling me about how people who have inherited diseases should just be euthanized. That was probably next.

"It's not just genetic diseases," he said, gesturing his hands wildly. "It's that, how can I say this, the only people who will be able to afford human cloning in the future will be persons of means. I know that you probably are aware there's a link between low intelligence and poverty. If only people of means were allowed to reproduce, then we'd have a utopian society, where everybody is contributing towards the good of the whole. Nobody would be on welfare, nobody would be on food stamps, nobody would be on disability. Everything would be pulling their own weight. I think you would agree that such a society would be a much better than the society we have now."

I wasn't exactly sure what he was getting at. "Are you saying that your dream is to have a society where only human cloning is the way people reproduce? No one else will be able to have kids the normal way?"

He chuckled a little bit. And then he took a swig of his wine. "Oh, if only that was possible. But no, everybody thinks in this world that everybody needs to reproduce at random. This is what they want. No matter what kind of genes you're passing on, no matter how little money you have to care for a child, it seems to be everybody's right just to have kids they can just destroy. I don't believe in that. I believe that is the kind of mentality that has destroyed our society. I'm working towards correcting that. That's all I'm doing. Correcting it."

As he was talking, I was thinking I'd have to try to get some of the internal memos of the Pegasus company. Something was forming in my brain, an idea. An idea about maybe who actually killed Lawrence. And why.

But the idea was only that. An idea. It wasn't something fully formed, but maybe it could become fully formed if I could get some information on the company.

I interviewed him a little bit more. I was also really interested in his twin studies, but on that subject, he wasn't as forthcoming about what those studies entailed. He simply said he was in charge of studying identical twins separated at birth. One twin went with one of the parents, the other twin went with the other parent. He was thus able to examine how genetics played on the personalities, intellect and so forth of the kids, and how much was the environment.

I drove home from that interview feeling depressed. I didn't want to believe there were people like this doctor in the world. People who didn't value life. Well, that wasn't necessarily true. He did value life, just not life that was imperfect in some way.

If only society could get rid of people like him, we'd probably all be a lot better off.

Chapter Nineteen

WHEN I GOT BACK to the office, I saw a woman sitting in the suite. She was a tall woman, redhaired, probably around 50 years old. She had the high cheekbones and wide face of an Eastern European woman. Blue eyes, delicate nose. Red hair.

She looked vaguely familiar to me. I just glanced at her, and headed back towards my office. I just figured she was there to see somebody else. But our receptionist, Charlotte, stopped me before I could get to the office.

"I think you want to talk to this woman," Charlotte said, motioning to the woman, who was reading through *People* magazine on our leather couch in our . The woman glanced up at me, and then looked at the tropical fish swimming in an enormous tank at the far end of the reception area. Then she looked back at me.

"Charlotte, I would love to talk to this woman. But I have a lot of work to do."

"No. You don't have that much work to do. In fact, if you speak with this woman, I think you'll be a lot further along in your work then if you don't talk to her. Trust me on this."

I rolled my eyes. "Okay, you got me. Who is this woman?"

"Her name is Olga Vasiliev. She's Marina's mom."

Chapter Twenty

"MARINA'S MOTHER? Marina is an orphan. Her parents were killed in a car accident when she was three months old."

"I don't know what to tell you, but she says she's Marina's mother. I don't necessarily know that she told me the truth, but if she is telling the truth, I think you need to talk to her. Now."

Come to think of it, that was the reason why this woman looked so familiar. She did look exactly like Marina, only about 20 years older. She looked like how I imagined Marina would look when she was about 50.

"Okay, this better be good. Send her into my office."

I walked back to my office. Charlotte stood up and I saw her motion to the woman on the couch, who also stood up. She was wearing a pair of Chanel sunglasses on top of her head and was dressed extremely well. Leather boots, black pants, silk top. She was carrying a handbag that I knew was an Hermés. I knew that particular brand, because my sister coveted it but could never afford it. At least, she didn't want to pay for something like that. Because of Avery, I knew those bags were about $15,000 and up.

I was confused about this entire situation. All I knew was that this woman looked like she had money.

She came into my office, and sat down. "Thank you very much for seeing me, Mr. Collins." Her voice was low pitched and thick with a heavy Russian accent. "You have to excuse my accent. I tried hard for many years to get rid of it. But I just can't seem to. I hope you can understand me."

"Yes, that's not a problem, but I'm curious as to exactly what I can do for you at this point."

She took a deep breath and then picked up a paperweight I had on my desk. It was a paperweight I'd gotten from The Air and Space Museum. It was a little tiny spaceship inside of a glass cube.

I noticed her hands were shaking. She brought one bony hand up to her eye and wiped away a tear. I silently handed her a box of Kleenex, and she gratefully took several, and then used the Kleenex to wipe away more tears. She sniffled a little bit.

"I'm confused as to what's going on here," I said. "Marina told me her parents were dead. Killed in a car accident when she was a little girl. Now, here you are, telling me you're her mother." I shook my head. "I'm skeptical about this entire thing."

"Of course, of course. You are right to be skeptical about me. If you need me to take a DNA test, to prove that I am her mother, then you are welcome to it. Whatever you need to do. All I can tell you is that I am not lying about this. I am Marina's mother."

"Does Marina know you exist?" I thought the answer was probably no, considering the fact that Marina said her mother was dead. Then again, maybe Marina lied about that, too. I didn't know what to think.

Olga shook her head. "No. She doesn't know I exist. I could never have the heart to tell her about what happened. Why I gave her up. Her and her identical twin sister Oksana."

"She has an identical twin sister? Does she know about her?" I asked. I'd spoken with Marina many times, and she never mentioned the fact that she had a sister. I wondered if she knew about the sister.

"I don't know if Marina knows about her sister. She probably does. But they have not been in each other's life since they were three months old."

"Okay, tell me the story about how Marina ended up in the orphanage and how she didn't know she had a sister."

Olga nodded. "Okay, here's the story. I was living in Leningrad, which is now called St. Petersburg, right before the fall of the Berlin wall. It was a time of major upheaval. Poverty, many people didn't have a job. People living on the streets. I didn't have enough to eat, and I didn't have enough food to give my children. I tried hard to find a job. My husband, Vladimir, was killed by the KGB, for reasons I still don't know about. He seemed to have some kind of secret life. We were broke. Vlad was the breadwinner, and when he died, we didn't have a way of bringing in money. I had two little girls who were two months old when their father died." She took another breath and then asked for another Kleenex, which I gave her. She dabbed her eyes and blew her nose. Her hands were shaking.

"So, I had two little girls at home, no husband, no job, we were all starving. The two little girls, they were wasting away. I didn't really care about myself at that point. I just wanted a better life for them."

"Okay, that's understandable. So what happened?"

She shook her head. "A man came. He came to see me. He told me he heard about me from some underground something or another. He said he heard about me through the streets, the grapevine, as you say. He told me he knew what position I was in. He told me there was a way I could have a better life of my children and for me."

Her voice started to crack, and she took the Kleenex and started to twist it around and around. She took a deep breath. "He told me that if I let him have my children, he would make sure they were placed in excellent homes. He would make sure they were well taken care of. I could start over here in America, with a lot of money. Enough money to last me for the rest of my life. But only if I decided to give him my children."

She brought her hand to her lips and started to bite her nails. She was shaking all over. She looked out the window of my office, and cocked her head slightly. She kept taking a deep breath, over and over again. As if she was trying to choke back tears, but it was no use. She started crying in earnest, taking one Kleenex after another, as she sobbed and wailed in my office. She sounded like an animal dying in a trap. The wailing, the howling, the eerie silence that came after it.

I waited for her to give me the signal she was ready to talk some more.

"Okay, here's what I really don't understand. Marina spent the first seven years of her life in an orphanage. If you gave your children to this man, and he told you he would take them and give them a good life, how did Marina end up in an orphanage?"

"I don't know the answer to that question. All I know is that I was desperate. I knew that if something didn't change, all of us would starve to death. All of us. There was no food in the house. No money to buy food. No clean water. There were rats in the street eating better than me and my children. All I know was that this guy was giving me a chance. My children a chance. I didn't really question anything. I wanted something for them and I couldn't give it to them. So, I gave this man my children. And he, in exchange, got me a passage to America and helped me get a green card. He helped me get my citizenship. He helped me start my life here in America. He gave me $50,000. That was, in my mind, more than I ever thought I would have in my life."

She looked me right in the eye. She was no longer crying, but she looked almost defiant. "I suppose you think I'm a terrible person. Selling my children like that. And I am. I am. I live with that for the rest of my life. My entire life, I have lived with what I have done. And, I will admit, I did not keep track of my children. I didn't want to keep track of them. I wanted to leave it all behind me because the guilt was overwhelming. Every single day, I would to see their little faces, and I would break down. Absolutely break down. I couldn't function. So I tried to detach. Disengage. That's how I didn't know that, all these years, Marina was in an orphanage, from the age of three months until the age of seven. I didn't know any of that, until-" And then she stopped.

"Until what?"

Another deep breath. "I saw her picture in the paper. It was as if I was looking at myself. She has my face. My eyes. My hair, everything. She's me. And when I saw her name in the paper, I knew she was the child I'd given up all those years ago. It broke my heart to find out what had happened to her over the years. I really did think that when I was giving her and her twin over to that man that they both would have a good life.

That man promised that to me. He gave me his word that he would make sure Olga and Marina were adopted out by a loving American family. And Marina, obviously she was not. I mean, she was adopted by a good family, but only when she was seven years old. I read in the paper about what she went through when she was little baby. When she was small child. What she went through in that orphanage. The sexual abuse, neglect, starvation. The physical abuse. I broke down when I found out about it. When I read all about her life in the paper, I just broke down. I couldn't take it. I couldn't take knowing that I was responsible for her having such a life. And here I was, living the good life in America. I met a nice man, a neurosurgeon, over at Sharp Hospital. We have an amazing life. But I couldn't pretend anymore that I did not have daughters. Not when I knew that one of my daughters ended up being accused of murdering her husband.

I also know she has a lot of mental problems. I hired a private detective. I know about the arson, the fights she has started, the assaults she has perpetrated on other people, all the times she's been arrested. I know that the reason why she turned out the way she did was because she did not have the love of parents, and in fact, all she had in the orphanage was abuse. From the age of two months until the age of seven, that's all she experienced. Abuse. And I talked to enough psychiatrists about her to know that when a child has a start like that in life, they don't have a chance. They're broken inside."

She was crying again. She licked her lips. And then looked out the window again.

"My daughter is broken because of me. And now I'm

broken too. I'm fractured too. I have a hole in my heart, just like she has a hole in hers. I can't look at myself in the mirror. Just the sight of myself in the mirror makes me sick. I can't stand the fact that I did what I did."

I tapped my fingers on the desk. "What about Olga? Do you know about her?"

She sighed a little bit. "Well that's just the thing. Olga, she was adopted out by a nice American family. That man, he brought her over to America. He arranged for a private adoption with a wealthy family on Fifth Avenue in New York City. She had the life that I always hoped both of my daughters would have. A father who's a psychotherapist, a loving mother who stayed home with her. They gave her everything I ever wanted for both of my girls. I don't know, I really thought that both girls would have gone to the same nice wealthy family. I really hoped that they would have. But they didn't. Obviously."

Her story was extremely curious. To say the very least. So, two little girls. One was locked in an orphanage, the other one was placed in a good home with a wealthy family right here in America. And there was a mysterious man who arranged all of it.

"So Olga, she was placed with a good family, right away?"

"Yes. That's right. She was. From the moment I gave her over to that man, she was with this new family here in America."

"Where is she now?"

"She's living here in San Diego. Living in a slum in the Barrio. She's posing as a boy and has a lot of problems too. She even changed her name to a boy's name. Brock. I guess she's into drugs. Meth. Addicted for many years now." She shook her head. "I don't understand it. Why did Oksana end up like that? She had everything."

I thought about Regina, and how she went to see a boy, a guy in Barrio Logan whose name was Brock. I wondered if it was the same guy. That actually made a lot of sense, because Regina could never understand exactly how this boy was related to Regina. Why Marina would be hanging out with someone like that.

I would have to talk with this Brock person. It was strange, though, but Regina didn't mention any kind of resemblance he had with Marina. Then again, if you live a life where you're addicted to meth, you lose all your teeth, you become extremely skinny, and if you are also transgender, it's understandable you wouldn't look the same anymore. So, just because this Brock person did not resemble Regina, didn't mean he was not the person who was formerly known as Olga.

"And, I'm so sorry, I know you said there was a man who arranged all of this for you. The adoption, everything. Can you tell me who that person was?"

"Of course. His name was Charles. Charles Weber."

Chapter Twenty-One

DR. WEBER? Suddenly, pieces of the puzzle were falling together. Coming together like crazy. I still didn't have the entire picture, but I had a piece of it.

"He's a scientist, isn't he?"

"Yes. He is a scientist. He is working over at this place called Pegasus. Doing twin studies. He's the head of that. I know he also knows a lot about what's going on with that company with their efforts to do human cloning. I find human cloning sick. I mean, I do understand that it's something that people want to do, in the future, just to say they've done it. You know, it's like going to the moon. It's of no use for anybody, but some people will want to have that done. Just because they want to make another version of themselves. Maybe because they think they're just so wonderful that there should be another one of them. That's the only thing I can think of. That's the only reason why anybody would do something like that."

By now, Olga was much calmer. I went over to the water

machine, and poured a glass of water for her, and one for me, and then I sat back down.

"I hate to say this, but I completely agree with you. I talked with this guy, and all that I can say is that the dude is way creepy. I think he wants to have some kind of a master race. And I think I know what happened to your daughters. I think I know why they were separated the way they were. And, I think I know the reason why Marina was left in an orphanage."

"Why? Why would that have happened?"

"I don't know for sure. But I think I need to talk to the adoptive parents of your other daughter, Oksana. Can you give me their phone number, addresses, anything?"

She went to get a pad of paper out of her purse, and wrote something down. "Here. Their names are Sylvia and Harry Jacobs. They live in New York City. They haven't spoken with their daughter in years. They have not kept track of her all these years. I know this because I contacted them when I tracked everybody down, my private investigator found them, Oksana and Marina and everybody. And so I was able to talk to them. They told me that Oksana is somebody they don't even know anymore. They haven't known her for years. But you can go ahead and talk to them if you think it can help you any."

"Are they somehow associated with Dr. Weber, by any chance?"

"Associated, in what way?"

"Did they know him?"

"I don't know the answer to that question. I really don't."

Somehow, I thought Jacobs probably did know Dr. Weber. It was obvious what happened – Dr. Weber was studying Marina and Oksana to see what would happen if one child was completely neglected, abused, physically and sexually, and not given any kind of love or care for the first seven years of her life. And then compare that twin with the other, who was given everything she wanted.

I had to admit, it seemed a bit ironic. The family that adopted Oksana were obviously people of means. They were smarter than everybody else, they had better genes to pass onto the kids, and I'm sure Dr. Weber assumed they would provide a better home than everybody else. But it seemed that, no matter what happened in this situation, no matter how many riches and privileges Oksana was given, she still turned out to be somebody living in poverty. She renounced her parents, obviously. And now she was living in a slum. According to Regina, she had no teeth, probably lost to meth.

I had to wonder exactly what the study of the Vasiliev twins told Dr. Weber and how he wrote it up. Marina was the one who ended up living in wealth. Granted, it was not her wealth. It was given to her, by her husband, and she was earning a large salary from him every year.

But she was living in a very nice home, surrounded by all the luxuries Dr. Weber would envy. And Oksana ended up in the slums.

I knew I needed to talk to the Jacobs to find out exactly what happened with the Vasiliev girls.

Chapter Twenty-Two

MARINA

MARINA HOPED that she told her attorney the right thing. She'd been in contact with her sister, well, she guessed Oksana was her brother now. Brock insisted she was no longer a she but currently a he. Marina could never wrap her mind around that, but she had to accept it, so she referred to Oksana as Brock and called him by male pronouns, like Brock asked for.

She'd been convinced for the longest time that Brock actually killed Lawrence. She had no idea, really, who killed Lawrence, because she genuinely was in a dissociative state at that time. She found out some information disturbing to her, more disturbing than anything could possibly be. Information that made her want to vomit. She simply could not understand somebody would do something like that to her.

Who would leave a baby in an orphanage deliberately, just because that person wanted to see how the orphanage would affect her? That person wanted to see how different she would be from an identical twin who was given all the advantages of life. It was evil. That's all that she could say about it. Evil.

She forgot how she found out what had happened. No, that wasn't necessarily true. She remembered how it happened. She remembered how she found it out.

Lawrence was careless. He had left his computer on a certain page and she saw the information there. She saw what Lawrence had written to Dr. Weber, and she realized what had happened.

She still remembered the day she found out exactly why she was in the orphanage all those years. Why she was not with a good family until the age of seven. By the time her adoptive family got to her, the Williams, it was too late. They tried to do all they could for her, but it was no use. She was so broken inside that there was just nothing they could really do.

She was broken because of what had happened to her in the orphanage, and what happened in the orphanage was directly the result of some evil, twisted thoughts in one man's head. Some evil twisted study. She didn't know she had a sister, let alone an identical twin, until she saw that email sent from Lawrence to Dr. Weber, even though she always felt in her heart that she did have a sister. But it wasn't confirmed until the email.

When she found out she had an identical twin, it was just a matter of doing some detective work on her own, hiring a private investigator to find out exactly what happened to her twin. Somehow, someway, she managed to track her down. Him down.

She tried to help him. She tried to give him money, because it is obvious he was more broken than even Marina was. Brock would never take the money. He told her he was happy exactly where he was, living in a tiny apartment with rats all around. It was disgusting to Marina. What was more disgusting was that he wouldn't actually take the money she tried to get him.

Marina was starting to think maybe her mental health illness was something inherited, because it was obvious her identical twin had severe mental illness as well. It was obvious there was something off about him. Not just the fact that he was addicted to meth, living in a slum, all of that. He just seemed very off.

Marina was therefore convinced from the time that she found her husband had been killed that her twin was behind it. No matter how many times Brock told her that he had nothing to do with it, Marina would never believe him.

She'd do anything to protect Brock, because she knew that if Brock killed Lawrence, he was doing it from some kind of misguided sense of loyalty to her.

However, she finally started to believe that maybe Brock had nothing to do with it. She didn't know who killed her husband. She was recently sure that she didn't, although she could never be sure of even that completely. She was also reasonably sure it wasn't Brock.

So who killed Lawrence? She didn't know, but she was confident her attorney would find out.

Marina knew she wasn't going to a mental institution for the rest of her life.

She just had to hope Aidan could find out who killed Lawrence, and could find it out on time. She knew he had only 60 days to change her plea from an insanity plea to something else. Judge Watts had emphasized that if Aidan could not find the culprit, the person who killed Lawrence, then it was safer to go ahead with an insanity plea. A part of her knew this was true.

It would be horrible to go to a mental institution, possibly for the rest of her life. But, at the same time, she had walked down stays at various institutions her entire life. She could handle a mental institution.

It would be a tragedy to go to prison.

Chapter Twenty-Three

AIDAN

MARINA'S official arraignment was set for that Monday. I planned to make a plea of not guilty by reason of insanity, but first, I had to ask for a meeting in chambers. I needed to ask the judge what I could do in this situation, because I knew I'd maybe change my plea at a later date, once more information came to light. Because I was a newbie, I knew the judge would be willing to hold my hand through this entire process. This was important because I didn't really know what to do.

So, I and the prosecutor, Jenna Powell, who was a veteran prosecutor and knew what she was doing – after all, there was the possibility this would be a death penalty case, so they had to get someone top-notch from the prosecutor's office to try it – met with the judge in her chambers.

"So, counselor, you wanted to meet with me before the arraignment?" Judge Watts asked me. "Go ahead, hit me with whatever you got."

"Well, here's the thing," I said. "As you know, my client

doesn't have a memory of the night in question. I would like to plead not guilty by reason of insanity. I want that option. However I cannot say with any certainty that she killed him. If I come up with any new evidence along the line that she was not the one who killed him, I would like to withdraw the insanity plea. I would also like that option."

Judge Watts looked over at Jenna. "Well, Ms. Powell, what do you think about that? This means you're not really going to know how to prepare for this case because you won't know if insanity will be on the table. However, I'm inclined to agree with Mr. Collins. In a case like this, where he's not really sure if his client did it or not, he should have both options on the table."

"Well, as you say, your honor, it's not really fair to me. I'm not going to know if I'm preparing for defending against an insanity case, or if I'm preparing for a regular trial. Is this going to be a case of dueling experts or will it be a regular case of proving the defendant did it? I need to know that well in advance. So I'd ask you to force the defendant to pick and lane and stick to it. Or at the very least, he's going to need to take the insanity defense off the table after, say, 60 days. If the insanity plea is still on table 60 days from today, the defendant is stuck with it. We can schedule the trial for six months out. That would give me plenty of time to make the necessary preparations for whichever kind of trial he'll be asking for."

"That sounds reasonable," Judge Watts said. "In your case, Mr. Collins, if you can't figure out if your client did or did not do it within the next 60 days, you're going to be stuck with the insanity defense. But I'll give you 60 days of investigation to see if you can come up with another suspect. Hopefully in those 60 days, you'll be able to piece together exactly what happened the night Lawrence Murphy died.

In the meantime, I'll schedule the trial for six months from today. Which puts us into January 15 of next year. Whatever you decide after 60 days, that's how I'm going to proceed with this case. Which means that if you want to keep your insanity plea in place, I will order the necessary evaluations and you're going to have to start looking for an expert to present to the jury, etcetera. So, for today, we're going to say she's pleading not guilty by reason of insanity. I may have to re-arraign her at another time, depending on what you decide. But let's just get this out of the way."

I took a deep breath. What was my client going to say today? How would she be? Was she going be the Marina who wants me to enter an insanity plea, or would she the Marina who would insist I plead her guilty? Maybe she would be the Marina who wants me to try the case and basically throw it. I didn't have any suspects I could point to the moment. I could find some in the future, but, at the moment, I was flying blind.

Marina was out in the court, sitting at the counselor's table, her hands clasped in front of her. She was looking down at the table. I came out, she looked at me, and I could see in her eyes that she was hostile. I didn't know what that meant, but I knew I would have to just do what I had to do.

"Okay, Marina, I –"

"You need to talk to the judge again," she said. "You need to go back and ask if I can plead guilty. I need to hear it from her I can't. You need to do that."

"We talked about this, remember?"

"Go back there anyway. I want you to try. I don't want to go through trial. I just want this to be over."

I shook my head. The judge was back on the bench. "Your Honor, can I have another conference with you in chambers?"

She looked over at Jenna and then back at me. Then she motioned to both of us "okay, counselors, let's go back in the chambers and talk about whatever Mr. Collins needs to talk about."

After we went back into the chambers, I took a deep breath. "My client wants to plead guilty. I wanted to know if that's an option here."

"I don't understand," Judge Watts said. "She wants to plead guilty? Can she make the factual basis for pleading guilty?" The judge asked me. "I'll be candid. The answer to that is no. Unless she suddenly got her memory back from that night and can stand up in court and answer questions about how she killed him, I won't accept a guilty plea."

"What about an Alford Plea?" I asked her, referring to the type of plea where the defendant pleads guilty, yet asserts innocence. This is used where the defendant knows the evidence against her is sufficient to convict.

"Obviously, it's her right to plead guilty under *Alford*, if she wants," Judge Watts said. "But I won't take a straight guilty plea from her."

"That's what I told her. So I'm going out there and telling her that a straight guilty plea won't be on the table anytime soon."

"Right," Judge Watts said. "Okay, let's get this over with. Time's a wasting. Not to mention the fact that I'm starving." She took out a pack of gum and popped a stick in her mouth. "When I can't get a meal anytime soon, it helps if I have my jaw working. Okay, you guys, let's get on out there."

All of us filed right back out into the courtroom, and I

went over to Marina. "Just like I thought. The judge won't accept a guilty plea from you. You can't get up on the stand and say you killed your husband when you don't know if you did or not. So she might accept a guilty plea in the future, but only if I can prove to her with facts that you did it. So, that's where we're at."

Marina sighed. "This is ridiculous. I don't want to go through trial. I don't want to have to go through a mental evaluation. I don't want to do anything. I just want to go to prison."

"Well, sorry, that's not going to happen today. Today we're going to do an arraignment. I'm going to plead you not guilty by reason of insanity. And in 60 days, if nothing has happened, and I haven't been able to figure out in my own investigation who killed your husband, assuming it wasn't you, then the not guilty by reason of insanity plea will stand. We're going to have to proceed that way. That's what the judge has decided. So we have 60 days to try to figure out exactly what happened."

"Well, then, I guess you know what you're doing. You're the boss."

"There is one other option," I said. "The judge won't accept a straight guilty plea. She will accept what's called an Alford Plea."

"What's that?"

"It's where you get up the stand and do not admit guilt, yet plead guilty to the charge. All you have to do is admit the state has enough evidence to convict you. However, I don't advise that, either."

"Why not?"

"Because I haven't even started the discovery process yet. I don't know that the state has enough evidence to convict you and neither do you. All I have is what's in the police report and the statement of information. If I plead you guilty through an Alford plea now, you'll come back on me for malpractice and can appeal on the basis of ineffective assistance of counsel. I don't want that following me around, so again, if you want to take an Alford plea right now, you can. But I'll have to withdraw from your case first."

And that was that. I suddenly made up my mind. If Marina wanted me to do something I knew was against the evidence, I would tell James to pound sand. I didn't need a black mark following me around, and I knew that Marina, whose moods and thoughts changed with the wind, would be just the kind of person who would sue me for malpractice if I pled her guilty before the facts were in.

She simply nodded when I said that to her. "Okay, you're the boss."

Her shifts in mood and tone were starting to give me whiplash. One moment, she was fighting me every step of the way. The next moment, she was willing to acquiesce to anything I wanted.

But I could see in her eyes that she was calculating something. I didn't know what it was, but there was something behind those eyes that made me think she would throw a monkey wrench into the gears.

I just had to shake off the feeling I got when I looked at her. Her face was blank, for the most part. But I could see in those eyes, just right behind those magnetic blue eyes, her wheels were turning.

The judge got on the bench, called the case, and I went forward with Marina. Jenna was up there as well. I pled Marina not guilty by reason of insanity, the judge accepted it, she announced to the court that we had 60 days to withdraw the insanity plea, and after 60 days, if the plea wasn't withdrawn, that was how the trial would proceed.

I was just happy to get through this part of the proceedings. I was not happy, however, with my feeling that everything would get messed up. FUBAR.

I had no clue exactly how it was all going to go FUBAR. I only knew it would.

Chapter Twenty-Four

THE NEXT DAY WAS SATURDAY, and I didn't have anything planned for the day. I only knew that, for once in like, forever, my weekend was my own. I hadn't toked up in quite awhile and I was itching to get to the pipe.

I went out on the balcony, lit up my pipe, and took a deep hit. The smoke burned my throat and my lungs as I inhaled forcefully. I remembered when I first started doing this. I was only 16. I was running with a crowd who smoked a lot of pot but I never did. I was drinking beer by the time I was 13, but I wasn't smoking pot at all at that time.

One of my friends, I think his name was Toby, finally decided it was time for me to get with the program and toke it up with the rest of them. At that time, marijuana was legal for medicinal purposes but not for recreational purposes. Now, of course, it was legal for everybody.

"Here, dude," he had said to me, passing me his joint.

I just shook my head. "No man, I don't do that shit."

He gestured to the beer I had in my hand. "You'll do

this, yet you're going to smoke weed?" he said, motioning to the beer. "Trust me, this is much better for you."

I had no desire to even try it. At that time, I bought into the whole story about how when people started smoking weed, it made them lay around the couch all day long, eating Nacho Cheese Doritos by the bagful. Somebody would ask a stoner a question, and they would just stare at the questioner and not answer. 10 minutes later, they would come up with a reply. That was how it was with every stoner I knew at that time. I had no desire to be one of them.

I finally decided to take a toke, of course. And I realized my body did very well with marijuana. It didn't make me want to just lay on the couch and eat a lot. It didn't make me feel like I couldn't function. It just made everything come into focus.

I've been hooked ever since.

I sat on the balcony and took another hit on my pipe. I put my feet up on the railing and leaned back in my chair. Our condo was facing the beach, and, it being a Saturday morning, there were a lot of people down there. I watched a volleyball game, and I watched all the people on the boardwalk below, doing their thing. In the distance, I could see the surfers and I knew I would be out there soon.

But, for now, I had to just chill. I thought that maybe if I toked up, I could see my way around this Marina case. It was baffling me, the way she was acting, the way she was changing her mind every five seconds about things, and just everything about it. I knew there would be problems in this case. I just didn't know what they would to be and how I would overcome them.

I hated that I didn't have an investigator anymore and I really hated that I didn't have an excuse to be close to Regina. I was looking forward to having Regina on the case, because I wanted to be close to her. I wanted to be close enough to touch her skin. Close enough to look into her green eyes. I wanted her to work with me, side-by-side, because I wanted to be with her.

Avery came out, with her dogs, Harlow and Lola. They were two boxer dogs, a year and a half old, and, like all boxers, they were hyper as hell.

"Hey, Aidan," Avery said to me. "I thought I'd find you out here."

I nodded and took another hit off the pipe. "Yeah. I may be getting out there pretty soon, surfing with the guys. But I have to think about what's going on with my case. I don't know, got me kind of rattled. My client has got me rattled."

"What's got you rattled? Maybe I can help?"

"Well, it's just kind of overwhelming, to be honest with you. I know this is the only case I have right now. When my firm assigned this case to me, they told me they didn't want me overwhelmed, so I don't have any other involuntary commitment cases on my plate at the moment. I guess what I'm saying is that this is the only game in town for me. And I feel like I'm going to blow it."

"Why do you feel you're going to blow it?" she asked me.

"I don't know. It's just that my client is not exactly mentally balanced. Every moment, it seems like she's trying to tell me to do something else in her case. Plead her guilty, plead her not guilty by reason of insanity, don't plead her not guilty by reason of insanity, try the case as a SODDI case. Some other dude did it. It just seems she's taking me on a roller coaster, a Tilt-A-Whirl, and I don't know what's going to happen next."

"Well, you just have to methodically investigate this case,

a little at a time. You know what they say about how you how to eat an elephant - one bite at a time? That's what you need to do with this case. Just take it one bite at a time."

"I guess so. Anyhow, I've been doing a little research on this Pegasus place. And you know how they're focusing on trying to get a cloned human being. Right?"

"Yeah. I understand that. And I think that might be what's behind Lawrence getting murdered."

"I think you're right. I have to wonder how it is tied into it. I've been trying to find out information about what kind of human subjects they have been taking on, if any. And, so far, I've come up empty. Regina told me about a lady named Helena Maxwell who had a daughter, Genevieve, who she wanted cloned. But I can't find info on this. I put Christian on the task of hacking into the database, and he told me there hasn't been any movement on the human cloning front at all. All I know is, they're trying to figure out how to do it. But there is something I came across, that was, shall we say, intriguing."

"What was that?" Avery asked.

"Well, I guess that one of the studies that Pegasus has commissioned has been twin studies. And it makes sense, since there is so much interest in cloning a human being. It makes sense they would be looking into the nature versus nurture question. Because, if you think about it, what does a person want when they want a cloned human being? Let's just say you had a daughter. That daughter was killed in an accident. And let's just say it's 20 years in the future, or however far in the future it is that there'll be an actual human clone. You take some DNA over to the laboratory, because you want more than anything to have your daughter back. You don't want it to be a different kid, you want your daughter back."

"This is just a thought experiment, right?" Avery said.

"Of course it is. As I said, it sounds like Pegasus is not exactly moving along too quickly with finding human test subjects for human cloning. But it will become a reality at some point in the future. So let's just say that it's a reality. What would you be worried about if you wanted to have your daughter cloned?"

"Obviously, I would be worried my daughter wouldn't be my daughter, exactly. That she would look exactly like her but wouldn't be her. She'd be different."

I touched my nose and pointed at her. "Exactly. You would be worried she would be different. Because, even though she would have the exact same genetic code as the dead kid, she would have different experiences. That's the reason why in that movie and the book, *The Boys from Brazil*, they made sure they killed the kids' fathers at a certain age. They wanted to re-create all the conditions that created Hitler. So you would be concerned that you would pay all this money, probably hundreds of thousands of dollars, to have your daughter back, but she would be a totally different person. Just like when you often see identical twins and they're completely different."

"Right."

I shrugged. "So, the twin study seems to be of a piece with the cloning venture. It seems that Pegasus is really interested in the impact of nature versus nurture. That's always been a question, hasn't it? They want to see what kind of impact nurture will have on people, to see how much they can give somebody who would be asking for a cloned child, if they can give their actual child back, or if they could not do that because the nurture component is just too strong."

"I see. And why are you're talking about this?"

"I don't know. This is something that's been rolling around in my brain. I mean, a lot of places conduct twin studies. They're able to find twins separated at birth and study them. Pegasus is not unique in that way. Not at all."

I took another hit on my pipe and then watched the waves.

"What else are you thinking about with this case?"

"Not much. I just need to think about it. In the meantime, I'm going to get my ducks lined up in a row in case the insanity plea will be how I'm going to try this case. The judge gave me 60 days to figure out if I wanted to try for an insanity plea or if I wanted to try it a different way. So I have to find out, in a hurry, if there was some other person who might have had motive to have killed Lawrence."

"What do you have to figure out?"

"Well, here's the thing. Marina's therapist told me she had a business arrangement with her husband. I'm not breaking confidence in telling you that, because Marina herself told me that. He paid her a million dollars year just to be married to him. I've always thought that was extremely odd. Don't you?"

"Yeah, I guess so," Avery said. "But, then again, maybe not. Sometimes men marry women for their looks. You know, trophy wife and all that."

"Yeah, I know what you're saying. So why pay her? It's not like a normal thing where she's married to him, and you know, she's spending his money, right and left. Because she's a gold digger and all that. This is entirely different. She was getting a salary just for being married to him. I think it's extremely odd. And I just can't quite put my finger on exactly why."

Avery looked like she was thinking about that one for a

second. "Well, let's see what the possibilities are. The two of them were married because —"

"I don't think she loved him at all." I didn't want to tell Avery about what the therapist told me about how Marina did not form such a strong attachment to her husband that she was afraid he would abandon her. Marina was desperately afraid of being abandoned, but not by her husband. She apparently didn't care enough to fear him leaving her. I thought the lack of emotional attachment she had for her husband was another odd thing about her marriage.

"Okay, let's brainstorm this," Avery said. "It could just be what she's saying. Her husband wanted to hire her as his wife, in effect, because maybe he's gay and he just wanted a woman to look good on his arm when he went to cocktail parties and that sort of thing. You know, a lot of high-powered men want that. Especially if she can play the part, as Marina apparently can. Because, you have to admit, she has a certain charm about her."

"True that. She has a certain charm, but only when she's on. She also has a wicked, evil side to her and I don't think she can control it. In other words, Lawrence had to be always afraid that if he took her to a party, she would bring out the banshee, the Malphas. That's what she calls her demon."

"Malphas? That's kind of odd. I mean it's odd that she's so self-aware that she knows she has a very dark side. A lot of people in her situation don't see their dark side, or they don't want to admit they have one. They think they're perfectly normal. But you're telling me Marina believes she has a shadow self?"

"That's exactly what I'm saying. She knows she has a dark side. Quite frankly, I don't know which side is the real Marina. I think they're both her. Anyhow, I'd think the possibility that she would all of a sudden just start screaming and yelling at people at a cocktail party, for no good reason, and breaking things, would be a deterrent for her husband to want to take her anywhere. So, in other words, I don't necessarily think she would be the best candidate for somebody who was just wanting to have a piece of eye candy on his arm. A guy like that can certainly find somebody who's, shall we say, a bit more sane? So, I'm not buying it."

"Okay, let's just think of something else. Let's think about the good reasons for the marriage and then we'll try to think about the bad ones. Okay. Let's just think about the possibility that maybe Lawrence took pity on Marina. Maybe he was friends with her adoptive parents and they explained to him that she was a Russian orphan, all of that. And maybe he just had a special place in his heart for someone with a sad story. Maybe her situation just made him feel bad, so he decided to take her in. You know, taking in an orphan. Some guys are like that. They have a savior complex. They want to be somebody's hero."

"No, I don't think that's the situation," I said.

"Why not?"

"Because, from everything I've heard and read about him, he's not the kind of guy who'll have a soft heart for an orphan and take her in just for that reason. Besides, I kind of get the feeling that maybe the two of them were not emotionally connected. I know they apparently had sex, because they had different sexual partners in their marriage with them. I just didn't think there was an emotional bond between the two of them. It doesn't seem that she cared for him at all. I don't know, maybe if he was trying to be her savior, maybe she just let him do it. I guess that might be a possibility. I just don't know."

"Okay. Let's think of something else."

"Here's what I've been thinking."

I took a long hit on my pipe. I was thinking clearly that morning, more clearly than I had been in a long time.

"I think she had something on him. I think she was blackmailing him. That was the reason he took her in and paid her a million dollars a year. To keep her quiet. That's what I think happened."

Avery nodded. "That sounds right, to be honest with you. That sounds more like human nature than my other ideas. I just wanted to get the good scenarios out there first, before we figured out if there was something that was not such a nice scenario."

"But why wouldn't she tell me the truth?" I asked.

"Because if she told you the truth, that she was blackmailing him, you might suspect she killed him. Maybe she doesn't want that."

"But she does want that. She wants to plead guilty." I took another hit. "Well, strike that. She's all over the map. I think the real Marina, if she would be really honest with herself, doesn't want to go to prison or to a mental institution. I think she's terrified underneath it all. So, yeah, it would be self-preservation for her not to tell me the score on that."

Avery nodded. "I think you might be onto something there."

"Well, it makes a lot of sense. And it kind of sticks a fork into all of my theories I had on this case."

"What do you mean?"

"Well, one of the theories I had was that Marina killed him but she didn't know what she was doing, because she was dissociated. And I still believe there was dissociation. On her interrogation tapes, she was acting really bizarre.

Like the cops asked her questions, and she would come back with something out of left field every time. Her face had a really flat affect, too. So now we're going to think that Marina killed her husband because she hated him. Whatever she had on him was making her angry, maybe angry enough to kill him. If that's the case, then I have to accept that maybe she killed him in cold blood. That would mean she was lying to the cops that she had no memory. It also would mean that she was acting when the Dr. Miller examined her and declared she was in a dissociative state when she was arrested."

"Yeah, I know what you're saying."

"And here's the other rub about that. Why would she kill him? She was married to him for the past seven years, quietly accepting his million dollars a year. If this $1 million a year is hush money and she was living her life and getting paid every year, why would she want to cut that payment off? Why would she want that to stop? She wouldn't. She would have to know that if she killed her husband that she not only wouldn't keep getting the million dollars year, but she would also be cut out of the rest of his estate. Both because she can't profit from the estate of a person she killed but also because Lawrence didn't leave her anything in his will. Nothing. Not one penny. She had to have known that was the case, that she would be cut off from his will.

So, all she has is the money she put in the bank over the past seven years – $7 million. So now what? I mean, it's enough for her to live on for the rest of her life. Comfortably. If she got out of jail and can beat this charge, she can buy a halfway decent house in this area with cash. And you know how these houses go up in value, so it would be a good investment for her. She wouldn't have to worry about money again. But, at the same time, if Lawrence would've lived, she would've kept collecting money every year. Why cut that off?"

Avery nodded. "Maybe she killed him and figured she would beat the rap and could live off the money he'd given her over the years without having to worry about answering to him anymore. She would have freedom from him and a lot of money to boot. That's a win-win for her."

I shook my head. "No. That doesn't make any sense, considering everything that's going on. She alternates between wanting me to plead her guilty and pleading her insane. If she's found not guilty by reason of insanity, she'll be committed to a mental institution, probably for the rest of her life. If I plead her guilty, she would go to prison for the rest of her life. On occasion, she tries to tell me that she wants to go to trial and try to beat the rap altogether. But usually she's trying to get me to do one or the other – not guilty by reason of insanity or straight-up guilty. In other words, she's not trying to beat the rap."

"And if she wanted to kill him to get him out of the way so she could just lead her life–"

"She would not only want to go balls to the wall, she would've hired a shark, not somebody who had never tried a murder case in his life."

"True," Avery said. "So, what do you think?"

"I don't know yet. I don't know yet. There's something I'm missing with this entire thing. I feel like it's staring me right in the face, to be honest with you. I just can't figure out exactly what it is."

Chapter Twenty-Five

"AIDAN, I THINK I WAS FIRED," Regina said to me when I went over to her condo to ask her if she would be willing to go to New York City with me. I knew she was fired, not that I wanted that. But I wanted to do nothing more than spend the weekend with the woman I was falling in love with, and show her around, because I knew she had never been there before and I had been. Several times. Not that I knew the city like the back of my hand, but I had a good grasp on the subway system, which was half the battle in that city.

I had been thinking about her almost all the time. I could not get the thought of waking up next to her beautiful naked body out of my head. I was going out of my mind trying to figure out how to make that happen again. So, when I decided that I would visit Sylvia and Harry Jacobs, and they agreed to meet with me, and I got my plane ticket to New York City, I knew I wanted to have a companion there. The companion I wanted was Regina.

"You have been fired, but I was kind of hoping that you would go with me anyway," I said. "I would treat it like a vacation for you. I know you've never been there before, and trust me, you haven't lived until you've gone to New York City."

"Is there any money in this for me?" Regina wanted to know. She raised an eyebrow. "Listen, I know you're going to see people out there, talk to them. And trust me, you need someone to come along with you. But when I say that, I mean you need someone to come along with you and actually do some work. It's high time that you talk to your client about rehiring me. Because if you just want me to go out there and swim in some kind of rooftop pool, tanning my ass while you gallivant around New York City talking to this person and that person, then you can forget it. I work for money. And that's it."

"Okay, I'll talk to Marina about re-hiring you. Listen, when she insisted that you were going to be off the case, she was in kind of a weird mood. You have to understand one thing about Marina – she's very changeable. Her moods are very changeable and so are her thoughts. Maybe I can catch her on a better day and she can talk to James about rehiring you. If she will agree to that, will you come with me?"

"Of course. I could use the cash. And, you're right, I've never been to New York City and it would be a fun thing to do. But I'm not going unless I'm getting paid."

So, I had to go and see Marina and see if she would be amenable to hiring Regina back. I also wanted to ask about Oksana. But not until I spoke with Sylvia and Harry and found out as much information from them as I possibly could. I had a feeling they were going to know much more about this whole situation than I thought they would.

I did my research and found out that Harry Jacobs was a psychotherapist with an office on Fifth Avenue. He apparently treated very wealthy people, for Harry was worth millions.

When I found out that the guy was a psychotherapist, my radar immediately pinged. Since he was a psychotherapist, he probably knew Dr. Weber and the two of them were probably in on this whole situation. At least, that was my feeling about it. I personally thought Sylvia and Harry Jacobs were probably as guilty as anybody, complicit in this entire scheme. However, I would reserve judgment until I talked to them.

I asked Marina to come to my office, because I wanted her to know what I found out. However, I didn't want to necessarily tell her I saw her mother. Olga told me that Marina still did not know of her existence. She still didn't know she was alive. Marina still thought, after all this time, that her mother had been killed in a car accident along with her father, Vladimir. I didn't want to tell Regina about her mother because I didn't know how she would react. It might break her to know her mother sold her. So, I decided to wait to tell her about her mother.

Hopefully I would get Regina back on the case, because I needed her to also do some research on Vladimir Vasiliev. Olga told me he had been killed by the KGB. That immediately had my alarm bells going off. The KGB doesn't just kill anybody for no reason. They kill people who were enemies of the state somehow, or who got on the wrong side of the president of the country. At any rate, I'd have to talk to her psychotherapist about whether or not I should tell Marina that her mother was alive. I certainly did not want to do that to her if that was something that would destroy her even more.

Chapter Twenty-Six

I INVITED Marina to come to my office and she showed up the next day, to ask her if I could re-hire Regina.

She was smiling when she saw me. "You wanted to see me?"

"Yes. I wanted to see you. Listen, I wanted to ask you some questions about Regina Baldwin. She's the investigator I was using and you made me fire her. I would like to go to New York City to interview some witnesses and I want to take Regina along with me."

She lay back in her chair. "I don't want you to be having sex with her. I don't want you doing that, because I think you belong to me." As she looked out the window, it looked like she was absolutely serious when she said those things. "I had a dream about you last night. It was such a good dream. I think that after all this is over with, and, assuming I'm not in prison, or in a mental institution, I think you and I can probably make it work. Do you think?"

I shook my head. "Marina, I think we've gone through this before. You're my client, I'm your lawyer. There are rules about this sort of thing. And I don't plan on breaking them, not for you. Not for anybody."

She lifted her face and cocked her head, and kind of studied me, her blue eyes shining. "Well, you're going to come around to my way of thinking. I know you're going to. And maybe you need to get that other person, that Regina, out of your system. That's what somebody told me needed to happen here. I was talking to a friend of mine about you and me. And I told this person that the thought of you with that gorgeous woman, Regina, makes me feel nauseated. Sick to my stomach. It tears at my heart to see you around her. But my friend, she told me I can't hold on too tightly. I always hold on too tightly to everybody, and that's why they always leave me. I just try to grip them in my hands, keep them on a short leash, and they don't like it. So she told me I needed to let the leash out a little bit on you. Let you see the world and other women, and then you can understand you're supposed to be with me."

I felt defeated. I let out my breath. It was obvious that what I was saying to this woman was falling on deaf ears. She obviously had some kind of illusion that she and I were in a relationship, and there was nothing I could really do to tell her this was not the case. She wasn't going to listen to me.

But it did sound like she was willing to let me hire Regina back. Whoever was advising her told her it was best that she give me my freedom to do what I needed to do. Therefore, I would leap on that suggestion.

"So, it's okay for me to hire Regina back?"

She clasped her hands in front of her, and gave me a look that told me she wasn't happy about any of it, but she felt she would have to do it anyway. "I suppose if that's what you need to do to understand that I'm the woman for you and you're the man for me, then I suppose it's best you get her out of your system. So go ahead and hire her back. Do what you need to do. I'll tell your boss, James, that I'm okay with her being on your payroll."

And then she looked away.

"There's one more thing "she said to me. She scratched her cheek, and pulled on her hair. She ran her fingers through her silky red hair, and then put her hair up on top of her head for a second with her fingers, and let it gently cascade back down to her shoulders.

"What's that?"

"I want you to try to find the real killer. I don't want to be called crazy to the court. I don't want to go to a mental institution for the rest of my life, or for any of my life. Unless you can show that if I did kill him, it was because of temporary insanity. Then maybe I wouldn't have to go to a mental institution. But I'm beginning to think I didn't kill him. And I don't want to have to pay for it."

Once again, I felt like I was on a Tilt-a-Whirl. It seemed like every other day she was changing her mind about exactly how she wanted me to try this case. Plead her guilty, try to plead her insane, and now she was telling me she wanted me to look for the real killer, because she was finally convinced she didn't do it?

Why did I feel she was covering for somebody?

Or maybe she was covering for somebody before, but wasn't anymore?

"Okay. Thank you for allowing me to hire Regina back. I can guarantee the investigation will go a lot faster now. At any rate, I know you say you don't want to take an insanity plea, but, at the moment, that's where we are. Unless I can figure out exactly who killed Lawrence, to the point where

I'm convinced you didn't actually do it, then we are at the insanity plea stage. Still."

I waited for her to attack me, screaming like a banshee, or rip me apart, telling me she wanted me to do something else. I waited for her to change her mind, like she had been changing her mind all along.

Instead she just smiled at me and looked out the window. And then looked back at me. "Whatever you want to do. That's fine with me." And then she got her purse and got up. "Just let me know how you're going to pursue this. In the meantime, you know where to find me. Tata."

As I watched her leave, I was thinking about how strange it all was. But then again, her psychotherapist told me that was the way she was. She was hot and cold, on and off, with a shifting sense of reality and a shifting sense of self. Mood swings were just par for the course.

I called Regina. "Hey, Regina, we're good."

"Cool. I'll meet you at your condo, and we'll go to the airport together. Later."

"Later."

Chapter Twenty-Seven

REGINA CAME to my house on Friday afternoon, lugging a small suitcase behind her on wheels. I was impressed. I was used to women packing enormous suitcases for an overnight trip, because they had to have everything under the sun in these suitcases. All their makeup, hair products, flat irons, 18 changes of clothing, shoes, you name it.

But not Regina. She was just as low-maintenance as she ever was. I could tell that because her suitcase was so tiny, even though we were going away for the entire weekend. I made arrangements to see Sylvia and Harry the next day, Saturday.

Harry had told me over the phone that Saturday was the best time to see him, because it was his day off. He seemed like a good dude, a warm person. I was anxious to find out how they were able to adopt Oksana, and what relationship, if any, he had to Dr. Weber.

"Okay, Aidan, I'm ready to go. So let's call the Uber and get the show on the road."

I brought up my Uber app, punched in my information,

and the app informed me that an Alexander would be picking us up within the next five minutes. I knew we had to get a move on soon.

"An Uber is going to be picking us up, so let's go down and meet him."

I got my own packed suitcase out of the closet and Regina and I made our way down to the parking lot right in front of my condo. Within a few minutes a black SUV pulled up and I could see the person inside the SUV was Alexander. He looked just like his picture.

Alexander got out and helped put the bags into the back of his SUV, and we were off.

An hour and a half later, we were on the flight to New York.

"Now, tell me again what you hope to find out from these people?" Regina asked me after we took our seat and were in the air. I managed to get both of us First Class seats, which was a priority for me, considering the fact that this flight would be 5 1/2 hours long. I had no desire to have my long legs scrunched up in the regular cabin for that long. I just wanted to stretch out and relax.

"I need to find out how they were able to adopt Oksana. I'm also curious to find out if they knew Oksana had an identical twin. I don't know. Even though the guy seemed very friendly over the phone, I wonder if he has something to hide."

"Like what? What would he have to hide?"

"I don't know. I just kind of wonder if he's hiding his relationship with Dr. Weber, and I need for you to to look into this Vladimir Vasiliev guy. He's the father of the two girls. He was apparently killed by the KGB when the girls were only two months old, and I need for you to look into his background as well. There's something just not adding up in this entire scenario. I think if I can figure it out, I can probably solve the case. At least I can solve it enough that I can withdraw my client's insanity plea. But if I can't figure this out, all bets are off. She's safer going to a mental institution than prison."

"The plot thickens, to say the very least. I still can't believe that crazy doc would do that to those two girls. I mean, I've heard of this kind of thing happening. I saw this documentary called *Three Identical Strangers* about these three identical boys separated at birth, because some crazy researcher guy wanted to see how different they would be over the years growing up in three different households. The mother was a teenage mom and she put them all up for adoption. All three of them were separated, and none of the adoptive parents knew each boy had two other identical brothers. Each boy was given to a very different household. One boy was given to a blue-collar family, one was given to a middle-class family, and one was given to a rich family. This shrink guy, I think his name was Dr. Peter, and this woman, Viola, they wanted to study each of the boys to see how they reacted to the different environments. They didn't find each other until they went to college, and one of them actually killed himself."

I wondered how people could do something like that to somebody. Separate identical triplets, not tell the adoptive parents that they were getting at a child who had two other brothers. All because he wanted to study them?

But this. This was something else. This was far more evil than even that. This was deliberately leaving somebody in an orphanage and taking her sister and placing her with an affluent family, just to see how different they would be.

I sat next to Regina, quietly thinking about how I would

broach the subject with her about how I felt about her. She had to have known. I mean, after all, we did sleep together.

"Regina," I said to her. "I didn't just want you to come with me because I wanted to use your investigative skills with this family. I mean, that's part of the reason, of course. Because you're the best investigator. Nobody can read people like you can. You're the best with shaking people down. And I have to admit, that's partly why I wanted you to come with me. But it's only part."

She nodded. "I know, Aidan. Believe me, I know." She took a deep breath. "Aidan, I'm 33 years old," she began.

"I don't care about the age difference," I blurted out. "I really don't care about it. I know I'm 25 and you're 33, but it doesn't make a difference to me that you're older."

"Will you let me finish?" she asked in a very stern voice. "Geez. Let me finish. I don't care about the age difference either. It's only eight years, who gives a crap about that? That's not what I'm trying to say. I was just trying to tell you that I'm 33 years old and I've never had a relationship with anybody. Any man. Nor woman, for that matter. Unless, of course, you count Michael, my boyfriend/pimp back in the day. I went to live with him when I was only 13 years old, because, quite frankly, I needed somebody to take care of me at that time. And he did. In more ways than one. But that was the only guy I've been involved with in my entire life. I guess what I'm trying to say is, there's a reason for that. There's a reason why I don't get involved with anybody."

I knew what she would say before she said it. It was written on her face. But I went ahead and let her tell me whatever she had to say to me.

"See, I just have never had a good experience with a man. Aside from Michael, the only sexual encounters I've had have been with men who raped me when I was young and my johns from the days I worked the streets. The reason I became a prostitute was because I felt like that's all I was for men. Just somebody who they wanted to play with. They took it from me, whether I wanted them to or not, so I figured I might as well get paid for it."

I put my hand on her hand and rubbed it gently. She was shaking. This was more emotion than I'd ever gotten out of her. But, at the same time, it was also very discouraging. She was telling me exactly why she wouldn't be able to be with me the way I wanted to be with her.

"Anyhow," she continued, "When I went to prison for popping Michael, I really learned how to stand on my own two feet. I met some amazing women behind bars. Most of them have stories like mine. Tragic stories, but we had a kind of sisterhood behind bars. I went to all these classes in prison, too, about building my self-esteem and all that. I thought these classes would be bullshit. I had to go to these classes, they were mandatory and all that, and I thought I would go in there and just go to sleep. But, I was really surprised when I actually kind of took to those lessons. I would have to say prison was probably the best thing for me. If I never served time, I know I'd be dead."

"Have you thought about seeing somebody about your issues with men?" I asked.

She just shrugged. "I don't know. I've been afraid of seeing a shrink. A shrink would make me bring up stuff I don't want brought up. It's better to just keep it hidden, keep pretending it's not even there. So, that's it. I'm sorry about the other night. I'm sorry I got so drunk that you and I ended up where we ended up. You have to understand, that's the closest I've gotten it with anybody in years."

She started to laugh. "I guess it tells you something

about me. The only way I can get naked with some guy is if I'm three sheets to the wind. No offense. If I was actually somebody who was halfway normal, I would love to go out with you. I mean, look at you, you're gorgeous. And, you're probably the coolest guy I've ever known. Trust me when I tell you, there are women out there with much less baggage than me who can treat you the way you need to be treated."

Unfortunately, the things she was saying to me didn't make me not want to go out with her anymore. In fact, I felt myself growing even closer to her. She had confided in me and that meant a lot.

"Anyhow," Regina said, changing the subject. "Let's talk about what we're going to ask Sylvia and Harry Jacobs. What are we going to going to get out of this visit?"

I took the cue that it was time to move on from the earlier subject, as much as I didn't want to. I so wanted to talk to her about my feelings for her. But, at the same time, I didn't want to push her.

"Well, I just need to find out more about Oksana and I'm really interested in finding out exactly how they were able to get in touch with her. I wonder if they're somehow related to Dr. Weber."

"You think they're going to tell you about that?" Regina asked, incredulous. "I mean, if they were in on this whole thing, do you actually think they would come right out and say, 'yeah, I'm a willing participant in a cruel and evil experiment. I'm proud of it.' The answer to that is no. I don't think you're going to get what you want out of these people."

"I wanted to ask you about Brock. Were you at all aware that Brock was actually a female? And did you think he resembled Marina at all?"

Regina shook her head. "I'm embarrassed about the

entire thing. I guess I probably should've figured it out. But you have to understand, that kid, I mean, he's not a kid, he's in his early 30s, but he has been ravaged by drugs. Have you ever seen pictures of people who have a severe meth addiction? I see them on the Internet. Pictures that show the same person before an addiction, during it, and after they were fully addicted. Do you ever see those websites?"

"I know what you're talking about." It was amazing how much an addiction like meth can transform your looks. It makes you unrecognizable. I remembered seeing pictures of an actress by the name of Amanda Peterson. She was really pretty back in the 80s, fresh-faced, starred in a teen movie with Patrick Dempsey. By the time she died from a drug overdose, you could not tell that she was the same person at all. I had seen other pictures of people who suffered from a meth addiction, and the transformation in their looks was beyond belief.

"So what you're saying is that Brock, because of his drug addiction, did not look anything like his identical twin."

"Right. Combine that with the fact that looked like he had taken male hormones along the way, because you know, he looked like a guy and not feminine at all, and, yeah, to say he looked nothing like his identical twin would be understating the matter. But that's probably not exactly an abnormal thing."

"It's weird, however, that he somehow was on the list that Christian provided for you. He was somebody who was contacted by them through that sex site. I wonder why that would be."

"You mean, why was he contacted through the sex site, as opposed to contacting her directly? Like sending her emails, and calling her?" Regina asked.

"Yeah. I wonder why that would be."

"Well, maybe that's how they got into contact with each other for the first time. After all, it just showed they contacted him through the sex site only the one time. Maybe Brock had a different picture up, that happens all the time, and they contacted him for a rando encounter. Then he shows up, and obviously, they'd have no interest in that. But I would guess that there was probably some kind of psychic connection between the two of them and they recognized each other. That makes a lot of sense."

I tapped my fingers on the table in front of me. The flight attendant came around and brought Regina and me some drinks. I got a bourbon and coke and Regina got a gin and tonic. I picked it up and sipped it, stretching my legs a little bit.

"Yeah. That makes sense. So you think it was just a coincidence that brought them together? They just happened to hook up on the sex site, he gets there and Marina immediately recognized her as being her twin, even though she looked nothing like her, and she is currently a boy."

"Yeah. That makes a lot of sense."

I thought about that. However, something wasn't sitting right about that scenario. I didn't know quite what was wrong. It was just something in my gut.

The plane finally touched down after about five hours in the air, and Regina and I got an Uber to our hotel room, after going through baggage claim and getting out suitcases. Well, I guess I should say hotel rooms, plural, because I made sure she would feel comfortable about being out New York with me. I thought that if we had the same room, she would think I was being presumptuous and I didn't want that.

We were staying at the Four Seasons, which I knew was little fancy for her. But I didn't care. I was in New York City and I would be doing it right. Besides, my firm was paying for this trip. I would use their expense account in style.

I got to my room, threw down my suitcase and looked at my watch. It was noon and I had to see the Jacobs at 3 o'clock. So, I took a shower, and Regina went to her room, and, after 20 minutes, the two of us went and got another Uber car to have lunch before going to the Jacobs' house.

I was slightly nervous about seeing these people. I didn't know why. After all, I had a feeling they might be able to point me in the right direction as to where I needed to go for this case.

I guess I was nervous because I thought there was that possibility they would not be any help at all, which would make this trip pointless.

Well, not exactly pointless. I was out here with Regina. Even if she didn't want to have a relationship with me, I still enjoyed being close to her.

Chapter Twenty-Eight

AT 3 O'CLOCK, I was in the Upper East side apartment owned by the Jacobs. Sylvia Jacobs was slim and attractive. Early 50s. Black hair, pointed nose, dark eyes. She looked like somebody who probably was a runner, maybe, or someone who played a lot of tennis. She was definitely somebody who had kept in shape over the years.

Harry, on the other hand, was slightly overweight. Paunchy. He had a bald head and was short, about 5'6". He was wearing a yarmulke, it being Saturday, and he greeted the two of us with a hearty smile.

"Come in, come in," he said jovially as Regina and I approached the door to their enormous condo. It was overlooking Central Park, and it was extremely large, about 4000 square feet. I knew what apartments and condos went for on the Upper East side, and I knew this place was worth millions.

Not that that mattered but maybe it did.

Sylvia, like her husband, was anxious to talk to us. She let us out to the balcony, and she brought us all out some iced tea and a couple glasses, and some finger food - crackers and a little bit of kosher salami.

She poured a glass of tea for me and one for Regina. I took a bite of cracker and salami. Jacob was sitting across from me, smiling, and I felt more comfortable. It seemed like these people were not going to be hostile, to say the very least.

"I have to say, I was surprised you were able to track us down," Harry said. "But, at the same time, I'm really anxious to talk about my… son, I guess."

Sylvia nodded her head. "Yes, Oksana is now our son. And his name is Brock, not Oksana." She shook her head and looked at Regina and me. "Honestly, Harry's a psychotherapist. You would think he would have no problem with identifying our kid as a boy now. But you know what they say. Sometimes you can treat other people, but, when it comes to yourself, it's hard."

"Do you know Brock chose that name because he was such a fan of Barack Obama," Harry said. "But he spells it B-r-o-c-k. It's like he wanted to honor his hero but didn't want to go that far. He didn't want people to think he was weird. Because you know, in America, Brock is kind of a standard boy name. But Barack, that's still exotic. At least it's different for people not from Kenya. I mean whose roots are in the country of Kenya, not that I'm trying to say Barack Obama was from Kenya, because of course you know he wasn't."

At that, Sylvia started to laugh. "It happens every time. We start talking about our son and Harry doesn't know what to say. He starts babbling about this or that."

At that, Sylvia got up and came back out with a photo album. "Here, I wanted to show you how Brock looked before everything happened. Before she became a he, and before he, well, we lost him. We lost him, as surely as if he was dead."

She looked sad. I opened up the photo album, and, sure enough, when I looked at the the photos of the young Brock, I saw Marina. Exactly like she must've looked about 15 years ago. It seemed like the photographs stopped at the age of about 20. She had the same red hair, the same bright blue eyes, the same slim body, the exact same face. She was Marina, through and through.

"Are you aware that Oksana had an identical twin when you adopted her?" I asked her.

"Yes," Sylvia said with a sigh. "I did realize that. And so did Harry, didn't you, Harry?"

Harry silently nodded. He suddenly did not have a smile on his face. Rather, he looked lost in thought.

"And you were okay with adopting Oksana and not her an identical twin sister?" I asked her.

She looked over at Harry and Harry motioned her to be quiet. She nodded silently and I knew Harry would speak.

"Yes, I was aware of the situation. I can't say I was aware of what happened to Oksana's identical twin, but I was interested in the twin study Dr. Weber was doing. You know, I'm a psychotherapist and such studies have always fascinated me. I figured it might help me in my practice. Studies on the whole nature versus nurture thing are extremely important, vital even, because as psychotherapists we have to know how much genetics play a part in an individual's psyche and how much environment does. As you probably know, mental illnesses that are organic in nature, that come from the brain, or the body chemistry, those are treated differently than ones that are not organic in nature. I just felt the entire study of the twins was important. So, I agreed to allow Oksana to be treated like a lab rat."

"Harry and I had a lot of fights about that," Sylvia said. "I didn't want to have any part of it. But Harry, he said he wanted us to have a child, and that was only way he would agree to adopt any child. And I wanted a child, desperately. So if that was the only way I could get a child was to go along with separating twins, then I would do that."

Harry looked like he wanted to vomit. His face was just a little green. "I was a lot younger back then," he said. "I admit, I didn't think about the ramifications of what I was doing. And if I thought for just two seconds that Marina was just going to be left in an orphanage by herself, I would never have agreed to it. I was simply told that Marina would also get a home here in America. But they were going to place her with a home not as affluent as ours. That's what he told me. That's the only reason I went along with it. I really thought that Marina would also get a good home. But what happened, how they deliberately left her in the orphanage, and they deliberately made sure she was not adopted during her formative years, that was beyond the pale."

Now that was something new. I wasn't aware that the directive was that Marina had to stay in the orphanage for all that time.

"I'm sorry, what were you saying again? You said Dr. Weber arranged for Marina to stay in the orphanage for all those years?"

Harry took a deep breath. "Yes. That's what I found out. When I saw Marina's picture in the newspaper, after she was arrested for murdering her husband, I knew she was Oksana's long-lost twin. Obviously. Because she had Oksana's exact face. Not that Oksana looks like that anymore. Of course. As you probably know, Oksana has had her problems over the years. I'll get to that later, about how she went from being my beautiful sweet intelligent daughter to the person she is now. It's a tragic story, but not as tragic as Marina's story."

"When you saw Marina was arrested for killing her husband and you knew you had found Oksana's long-lost twin, what did you do?" I asked him.

"I read the newspaper article about her, just like anybody else would. And I read, just like everybody else, about her tragic back story. About how she was in a Russian orphanage for all those years and how she was sexually abused when she was a little girl in the orphanage. How she finally managed to find a loving home at the age of seven, but by then, it was too late. Her personality was already formed by then. The die was cast by that time. And that's true too, you know. A person's formative years, when they're one, two, three years old and so forth, those are extremely important years for forming a person's personality. When a child is that young and they learn the world is a scary place, that's the root of many personality disorders. That and the fact that if you don't get the proper amount of love and guidance at a young age and you fail to bond with an adult when you're very young, this is also the root of personality disorders. I also read she had been diagnosed with borderline personality disorder. I don't know where I saw that, but I saw it. And that makes sense to me."

"So how did you find out the orphanage was directed to keep her there for all those years?"

"Well, I have to say, when I found out the fate of Oksana's identical twin, I kind of went crazy. The fact that I adopted Oksana, knowing that she had an identical twin out there, had really been nagging at me all these years. I thought it was something I could live with, but it really wasn't.

But I always tried to comfort myself with thinking Marina had just as good of a life as we were providing for Oksana. When I found out the truth, I knew I had to go over to Russia and speak with the people who ran that particular orphanage. I wanted to find out why she was unable to find a home for all those years. Now I know the fact that she didn't find a home for so many years wasn't uncommon. Because of the adoptions rules and so forth and how international adoptions are so difficult anyway, I know there are lots of kids in Eastern Europe, Romania, Russia, Ukraine, so forth, who are in orphanages and not able to find homes. But I wanted to ask the adoption people myself, the people who run orphanages over there in Russia myself, about why Marina was unable to find a home. Because I had my suspicions."

"Suspicions about what?"

"I have my suspicions about Dr. Weber and his motivation. I knew he had lied to me about Marina being placed in a good home, so when I found out he had lied to me and Marina lived for so long in the orphanage, I started to think that maybe he was not such a good man."

Sylvia snorted. "You think? What was your first clue about that, Harry?"

"Sylvia, you know how I feel about all this. You know how devastated I am. So I really don't need comments from the peanut gallery on this. I beat myself up enough about it."

Sylvia waved her hand dismissively. "Okay, okay. You feel bad about it."

"I do. And that's the reason I'm anxious to talk to this gentleman and his researcher. I'm sorry, investigator. I'm anxious to talk to the two of you, because I feel responsible for what happened to Marina. If only I would've not gone along with it. If only I just would've insisted to the doctor that I would get both girls, or nothing, maybe that murder never would've happened."

"Don't worry about that, Harry," Sylvia said. "If you would've insisted that you were going to adopt both girls, the doctor would've just done it with two other identical twins. He would do it no matter what. That's just the kind of person he is. It's disgusting."

"I guess," Harry said. "I guess you're right. If he didn't do that work with Oksana and Marina, he would've done it with two other people. He was determined to separate twins and make sure one was in a horrible condition and the other one was in a really good condition. That was the study he wanted to have and that's what he did."

"So how did you find out Marina was supposed to stay at the orphanage for all those years?"

"What can I say?" Harry said. "That bastard, that Dr. Weber, he paid off the orphanage to make sure nobody could adopt Marina for seven years. Well, not exactly seven years, but 6 1/2 years. He wanted to make sure she spent her entire early childhood at this place. So when I spoke with the people at the orphanage, they told me that was their instructions. She was not open to be adopted to anybody. Dr. Weber made sure of it."

I bit my lower lip. That guy was truly a monster.

"And you've been in touch with Dr. Weber over the years, right?"

"Right. It was a longitudinal study, so we were required to answer questions about Oksana every year. We never told Oksana that she was the topic of a research study, though. We never wanted her to know there was another little girl around who was her twin. That would have devastated her.

I would imagine the adoptive parents of Marina did much the same."

"Do you know exactly why he would make sure she spent her entire early childhood there?"

"Of course. It all makes sense to me now, looking back. Oksana was a beautiful child. Friendly, outgoing, all of that. And I imagine that Marina was as well. I imagine she was the same kind of little child. Chances were that she probably would have found a home sooner or later. Probably sooner rather than later. And Dr. Weber just didn't want to take that chance. He didn't want to take the chance that Marina would have just been in the orphanage for a month or two, because then Dr. Weber would lose track of her, for one thing. And also, he wouldn't have gotten the data he wanted to have."

"Well, I guess that probably settles it. That guy, that Dr. Weber, he's truly evil." I thought about how Dr. Weber talked about how he wanted to have a master race, how he was in favor of eugenics and all that. Yes, he was exactly the kind of person who would do something like this.

I wondered if he managed to do a study like that to somebody else. He probably wanted to have several subjects, just like Marina and Oksana. It wouldn't do just to have the two.

"I wonder if he's had other subjects over the years, subjects put into the same situation?" I said aloud. "After all, just the study of Marina and Oksana won't yield anything significant to him. He had to have other people he was doing this with over the years."

"I'm sure that he probably did," Harry said. "Not necessarily from Russia, but probably identical twins from other poor countries that had children in orphanages. I would not be surprised if there are several other twins, or triplets even, who were put in similar situations. He was apparently studying the effects of being completely neglected, abused, and so forth, as opposed to having everything you ever wanted. And, the irony of it all, of course, is that we lost Oksana anyways. We gave her everything she needed in life. Sylvia stayed home with her, we gave her all the love she needed, we gave her tutors for school, and we put her in music lessons. We both spent a lot of quality time with her, reading to her, helping her with homework, taking her to playdates, everything. We made sure she had a good social life. We really made sure she was out with other kids, we made sure we had parties for her every birthday. She always invited all her little friends. We did everything for her and look what happened."

"I guess Dr. Weber's experiment failed after all, didn't it?" Sylvia said with a wry smile. She took a sip of her iced tea and daintily nibbled on some salami and cracker. Her legs were crossed and she was leaning back in her chair. It looked completely defeated.

For that matter, Harry looked just as defeated. Even more defeated, because he was the one who stirred his entire thing up.

"What happened to her, Oksana?" I asked him. "How did she become addicted to drugs?"

"The irony is that she became addicted to drugs in her private school. Turns out when you get a lot of kids in a school where there's lots of money, there's also lots of drugs. Not every kid gets addicted, however, but, apparently, our Oksana was prone to addiction. I should've researched her parents a bit better. If I would've, I would've known she would be a problem. Her father, Vladimir, was a drug addict himself."

Sylvia shook her head. "Senior year in high school and

Oksana was already becoming a different person. A much different person than she was before. She started failing in school, started losing a lot of weight, started really talking back to us. She started throwing a lot of fits, slamming a lot of doors, going up to her room, threatening to jump off her balcony. Several times. We put her in so many treatment facilities, so many of them. We spent a lot of money on these facilities, too. We put her in the ones that cost $70,000 a month and up."

"We put her in this place called the Dunes in the Hamptons. You ever hear about that place?" Harry asked.

"No, tell me about that place."

"It's $65,000 for the first 30 days, if that tells you anything at all. The people go out there and do yoga, meditation, hiking, they get massage therapy, acupuncture, and the best food money can buy. Lots of therapy. You go to that place and see sports stars, celebrities, actors, that sort of thing. That's the kind of place this was. She came out, started using again, so we sent her to Passages Malibu. Mel Gibson's gotten treatment there. David Hasselhoff. Natasha Lyonne. Anyhow, it's the same kind of thing, Passages Malibu. Just as expensive as the Dunes place, and, for our kid, just as useless."

"Now, Harry, you can't blame yourself for Oksana's addiction and I know you do," Sylvia said.

"Yes. I blame myself. I should have been figuring out she was buying drugs at school," he said.

"So she became a drug addict and you tried to get her into rehab a couple of times. Not just rehab but extremely expensive rehab. And how did she end up in San Diego?"

"I don't really know the answer to that question," Harry said. "All I know is that, one day, she was gone. We tried to find her. We sent a private investigator to find her. She was an adult by that time, 25 years old, but she just left her apartment we bought her in Soho, just left it, furniture and all, everything was left in that place. All her clothes, books, art work, knick-knacks, kitchen stuff, everything. But she was gone. And, I hate to say, we haven't spoken with her for the past five years."

"Has it been that long?" Sylvia said. "How time flies."

"Yeah, it's been that long," Harry said.

I immediately started to wonder about the possibility that it was all a coincidence that Oksana ended up in San Diego, the same city her identical twin lived in. Maybe I was wrong about the fact that the two hooked up through the sex site and they identified each other as being their long-lost sister.

"So you don't know why she went to San Diego exactly?"

"No. I have no idea why she ended up out there," Harry said, shaking his head. "I wish things were different. Obviously. But there's only so much you can do for your kid. You can only guide them along and hope they don't screw up along the way. She did, obviously, and now she's addicted to meth and is somebody I don't know anymore." He took a deep breath. "Have either of you seen her now?" he asked, looking at Regina and me.

Regina looked hesitant, as if she didn't want to tell him the condition Brock was in when she met him. She looked at me and shook her head. I guessed she wanted to spare them the details.

"No," I said. "We haven't been able to track him down, either."

"Well, I guess it's just as well," Harry said. "I would like to know Oksana is okay, however. Marina, too. Of course. I really hope you can find some way to get her off this murder charge. I feel awful about what happened to her. Just awful," Harry said.

"I do too," I said. "And we're doing all we can to make sure Marina doesn't serve time for this. All we can."

Harry reached over and grabbed my hand and gripped it hard. There were tears in his eyes. Sylvia's too.

"Well," Harry said. "I'm very sorry, but I have some work I have to do in my office. If there's anything else I can do to help you, don't hesitate to call, huh? And if you see Oksana, please tell her we love her very much. We desperately want her to come home."

We stayed around and talked some more to Sylvia, while Harry went into his home office. I realized that, after talking with her, and with Harry, that Dr. Weber didn't just destroy the lives of Oksana and Marina.

He destroyed the Jacobs too.

REGINA and I spent the rest of the weekend, just sightseeing in New York City. Doing all the things tourists do. Seeing all the neighborhoods, going to Broadway shows, going up in the Statue of Liberty, all that stuff. I was surprised Regina was so into it. She had always struck me as somebody who would be so above doing the tourist trap stuff. Somebody who would be just way too cool for any of that, but she seemed to have as much fun as a small child would have going to all the different museums, landmarks, and shows.

The Jacobs definitely gave me food for thought. That was definitely what they managed to do.

And they managed to open up a few questions for me too. Why did Oksana end up in San Diego, which just happened to be the city where her identical twin was? She must've known Marina was out there all along. But if that was the case, why hook up with Marina and her husband through a sex site? That was what really did not make sense.

I also needed to know one more thing. I would have to somehow, someway, find out more about Vlad Vasiliev.

Why did I have a feeling there was more to that guy than what anybody knew?

Chapter Twenty-Nine

MARINA CALLED me when I got back to San Diego. She wanted to share some emails she found on her husband's computer.

"Aidan, I need you to come over here and take a look at something. I was on my husband's computer. He always gave me his password, so it wasn't a big deal. I was looking through it, because I just had a feeling there was something I needed to know. It was something my friend told me I should try to figure out."

"Oh, really?"

"Yes."

I went to her house and looked at what she had to show me. And, just like that, I had an idea about exactly who did this.

And exactly why this person did this.

I also knew I would have to do one thing.

I would have to call a hearing and withdraw the insanity plea.

I finally had the answers I was looking for.

I finally had a good lead that told me my client did not kill her husband.

Chapter Thirty

I CALLED the hearing to withdraw her insanity plea the next Monday. "Counselor, I understand you might have some evidence that has led you to believe your client did not kill her husband?" the judge asked me when I went in there to tell her what I would do.

"Yeah. You might say that. However, I need to get permission from this court to subpoena some records from the victim's place of business."

The prosecutor, Jenna, was not keen on that.

"I know what records Mr. Collins wants to subpoena, and I don't agree with that at all. I think he's going on a fishing expedition, so I'm going to have to object to that," she said.

"Oh, I don't think you can object. You're going to want to see the emails I have printed out from my client's computer. Trust me, issuing a subpoena to the Pegasus company will be extremely important in this case."

I handed over the emails to the judge, and she looked at

them. "And you think there will be other emails on the company server?" the judge asked with curiosity.

"Yes. I believe so. This is just one email Lawrence had on his personal server. I don't even know why it was on his personal server, sent through his personal e-mail, but I would imagine there are probably some more official emails that the company has on their company server. And I would like to subpoena them."

The judge nodded. "I'll allow it. I'll sign off on the subpoena." She looked over at Jenna. "I know you object to this. Your objection is noted, but, I'll admit, if Mr. Collins can produce other emails that are along the same lines as this one, they're going to be highly relevant to the case. Good work, Mr. Collins."

When I got outside the courthouse, Jenna caught up with me. "Just what do you think you're doing, slandering the name of a good man?"

I snorted. "Good man. You don't know the half of it. You'll find out, at any rate, in the future, just how not good that man is."

I felt a little sorry for her. She was about to have her ass handed to her. By someone on his very first at-bat.

That would have to hurt.

Chapter Thirty-One

January 15 – the first day of trial

I WAS ready for my first day of trial, as ready as I could ever be. George bowed out of being my second-chair because James told me I didn't really need one, and George had plenty of his own cases he needed to worry about.

"I think you're ready for this," James said. He had reviewed the case with me, and I went over the evidence that I managed to accumulate in this case. He was impressed. "It's your first time out and I think you're good to go."

I was happy that I was reasonably certain that I could figure out exactly what happened to poor Lawrence. I could show the jury my client didn't do it. Because, really, when it came right down to it, Marina didn't have a motive to have killed him. Yes, the prosecutor's office would show that Marina had a motive, which was that she hated him. And, to that end, Jenna did have quite a few witnesses lined up who would be able to testify about just how much she hated her husband. But, at the same time, I thought my client's shitty words to her husband really didn't show motive to have killed him.

Marina didn't have motive to kill him. But somebody else clearly did.

Over these past few months, I learned that Lawrence actually was not a bad guy. In fact, he was a pretty good guy. I kind of assumed, after I found out about Dr. Weber, that Lawrence was probably a bad guy who was in on all of it. But I realized he really wasn't.

I was willing and eager to make sure I nailed the culprit to the wall. I want to make him squirm.

I got to the courthouse and Marina was already there. She was waiting for me outside the courthouse steps. The sun was shining on her hair, and she was dressed in a creamy white dress, with a blue and purple scarf around her neck. She looked almost like a lady.

"I know you're not supposed to wear white after Labor Day," Marina said, "but I don't think that applies in Southern California, do you?" She looked genuinely worried that she was dressed inappropriately, and I had to have a tiny chuckle about it.

"You're fine," I said. "You look fantastic, to tell you the truth."

She nodded, looking unsure about it. "I feel sick," she said.

"Don't worry, I got this."

"I know you do, but what are people going to say about me on the stand?"

"Well, it won't be good," I said. "You're going to be made out to be crazier than a hatter. Just be ready for it."

I had prepared her by telling her what witnesses were going to be on the stand. I had interviewed them and found out they had a lot to say. None of it good. Marina didn't seem surprised about the prosecutor's witnesses, of course. She knew what she did. She knew how she acted. When I told her about the state's witnesses, she seemed resigned.

Marina had actually started acting somewhat normal. I was still having problems with her, of course. She was still just as changeable as she'd ever had been. One second she was hot, the next second she was cool. But at least, once things started to settle down, she was not trying to get me to try her case in multiple ways anymore. She was no longer calling me every other day to say she would like to plead guilty, and then call the next day to ask me to plead her insane, and then back again.

She was no longer trying to direct traffic with this case, so that was a good thing.

I also found out the reason why she decided not to imagine a love relationship between the two of us anymore was because she met somebody. She had fallen in love with a woman by the name of Amber Hightower. I felt a bit sorry for Amber. I met her and she seemed like a nice, normal person. But she grounded Marina, as much as Marina could be grounded, so I thought maybe it could work.

Then again, Marina was Marina, so I didn't have too many high hopes.

But Marina did have high hopes. "For the first time, I've found somebody who might make me truly happy," Marina said to me. "I'm sorry for what I was saying to you earlier, about you and I getting together. I hate to break your heart like that. I know you probably wanted us to have a relationship. But, the heart wants what it wants, and my heart wants Amber."

I took a deep breath when she said this and tried to

suppress the hysterical laughter threatening to bubble up. She really seemed sincere when she was trying to "break it to me" that she and I couldn't be together, and I didn't want to hurt her feelings.

"I'm sad about that, but I understand," I said.

She nodded and then proceeded to show me her phone. There were pictures after pictures of Marina and Amber together. There they were at SeaWorld. There they were at the beach. Marina was sticking her tongue out in front of a building in Balboa Park. Amber was posing in front of a pissed-off looking sea lion minding his own business on a big rock by La Jolla Cove. There they were drinking margaritas in Old Town, raising their glasses to the camera with big smiles on their faces. There was Marina grinning at the camera while chimps played in the background.

It all looked so aggressively normal. I wondered how it could possibly be normal, but maybe Marina could control the crazy if she really tried.

All I knew was that, after Marina met Amber, things went much more smoothly in the case. I could finally focus on it without trying to worry that she would become obsessed that I was her lover and I better act that way.

As for Regina, things hadn't gone anywhere. Ever since our trip to New York, she was as good as her word. She rebuffed every overture I made that was romantic in any way, shape or form.

I got the hint. It just wasn't going to happen for me with Regina. So I went on dates with other women. We went to beach restaurants and bonfires, walking along the boardwalk, holding hands. A different girl every week, because that was kind of the way it was with me. My heart was with somebody else, and I just couldn't give it away to anybody else. Oh, I tried. I did try. But all I could think about when I was with all my dates was that I wished this person was Regina.

I just hoped the crush I had on her would go away.

But she worked on the case with me and she was golden as far as getting the documents and emails I needed to show what I think happened, and piecing them altogether.

I got up to the courtroom, and the judge was already on the bench. Jenna was already there has well, along with her second chair, Arnold Baker.

"You know, it's not too late to dismiss this case," I said to Jenna and Arnold.

"Not on your life," Jenna said. "Listen, I think you think you know what happened here, but I don't think you really do. Wait and see."

I didn't know quite why Jenna was so adamant that this case be tried, but it gave me a chance to shine.

It gave me a chance to show I had the evidence that my client was as innocent as a bird.

I just hoped I could prove it to the jury.

Chapter Thirty-Two

JURY SELECTION FLEW BY. I knew the kind of people I wanted on the jury, and, for the most part, I got them. Marina's story was a tragic one. As was Oksana's. I really wanted to find jurors who would sympathize with both of them, and I thought I did a good job of doing just that.

After talking with Oksana, who now was known as Brock, I knew that part of the reason why she became addicted to drugs was because there was always a part of her that felt like it wasn't there.

"I always felt like I was only half a person," he said to me. "I always felt there was another part of me out there in the world somewhere, and I didn't know how to fill the emptiness. I didn't know where the emptiness was even coming from. My parents never told me I had a sister, let alone tell me that I had an identical twin sister. That's the reason I refuse to talk to them."

I felt badly for Harry and Sylvia. They weren't bad people at all. But they were deeply flawed. Harry was guilty of being a little bit too eager to participate in a study that was clearly unethical. But, as I noted, if it weren't for them doing what they did, Dr. Weber would find someone else to do it with. It was just a matter of who.

Chapter Thirty-Three

THE PROSECUTOR HAD a whole host of people she would be calling. The medical examiner, the cops, some of the people from the sex sites who were going to testify that Marina and her husband had a relationship that didn't appear to be based upon love, plus a lot of people who apparently knew that Marina and her husband had a business relationship.

Through email evidence, I was finally able to find out exactly what was the basis for that relationship. And I finally knew that Lawrence was not a bad guy after all.

After the jury was chosen and they were sat, we were ready to begin. Jenna gave her opening statement, and I personally thought she had a weak case.

"Ladies and gentlemen of the jury," Jenna said as she addressed the jury. "This case is really not all that difficult to understand. You have a woman, Marina Vasiliev, who was married to a man who she alternately hated and loved. You see, that is the nature of what happens when you're married to somebody who has an unstable personality. You will hear evidence from individuals who were friends with the couple. They will tell you that they witnessed violence between the two of them. Violence where Marina punched, kicked, and verbally assaulted her husband in front of them. These same witnesses will tell you that they heard Ms. Vasiliev, on more than one occasion, threaten to kill her husband. You will hear evidence that Ms. Vasiliev saw her husband as somebody who was in her way. He was standing in the way of her finding someone she could truly love with all her heart. Because one thing is for sure. Ms. Vasiliev did not love her husband. No, it was a business relationship. Even she will tell you that on the stand. She will explain that she was paid by the year to be married to him. And she hated being married to him because, like everybody else in the world, she wanted to be with somebody that she loved, and she did not love him.

She might not have loved him, but she did love his money. Ms. Vasiliev was extremely greedy and was never happy with just the millions of dollars that he gave her over the years. She wanted it all. Everything. She wanted everything, all of his money, and she did not want to do anything for it. So she wanted all his money, but she also wanted to be with someone she truly loved. And, the evidence will show that she finally found somebody she truly loves - a woman. So, how would she ever have been happily married to Mr. Murphy if she was a lesbian?"

I knew Jenna couldn't state that my client had been diagnosed with Borderline Personality Disorder. Her diagnosis was something that I had managed to keep out through a motion *in limine* that I made to the court before the trial ever started. I told the judge that I did not want my client's diagnosis to be mentioned in court, especially because the psychotherapist who had diagnosed my client with that disorder was not going to be available for trial and, even if he were available for trial, he couldn't talk about Marina's diagnosis because of the HIPAA law. However, I also knew the prosecutor would show my client's instability through other ways.

Unfortunately, there were a lot of ways she could show that. She was actually correct. There were quite a few people who were privy to the dysfunction of Marina and Lawrence's relationship. Lawrence was a mild-mannered guy and Marina was volatile. And, yes, she had threatened to kill him in front of various people. There were also many people they met through the sex site. They had some regulars, and these regulars were the ones were going to testify on behalf of the prosecutor.

I knew there would be quite a few people who were going to talk about the violence Marina had visited upon Lawrence, the verbal threats she made to him, how she was constantly belittling him, always telling him she didn't want to be with him, that he made her sick and that she wanted to kill him. Yes, she said all those things. She admitted that to me.

Yet, I still felt I could overcome all of that because I had my ace in the hole.

At least, I hoped I could overcome all that, because it was a lot to overcome.

Jenna's opening statement went on for another five minutes. She went over all the evidence she would show them, and, I had to admit, she did not do a bad job.

My opening the statement was next, and I laid out what I would show them.

I knew the prosecutor thought she had the smoking

guns. Namely, all the vile things my client said to her husband, all the vile threats she made, and all the violence she had visited upon him.

I just thought my smoking gun was even better than hers.

Chapter Thirty-Four

AFTER BOTH OF us gave our opening statements, it was time to begin the trial. The first few people who Jenna would call were basic people who were going to state what had happened. The cops on the scene. The cops who interrogated her. And, the doctor who would testify that Marina had dissociated on the night of her husband's murder.

The fact of Marina's dissociation was part of Jenna's strategy. She wanted that evidence in court, because she wanted to make sure that Marina couldn't get up on the stand and state definitively that she didn't kill Lawrence. She didn't want me to put Marina on the stand to testify that she remembered the night of the murder and that she had nothing to do with it. So Jenna thought the best strategy to counteract that possible testimony would be to show that Marina had no memory of what had happened.

The cops gave their testimony about how they had come to the scene and found Lawrence lying in the foyer of their enormous La Jolla home, with Marina sitting in a chair in that same home, staring off into the space. They talked about how when they asked Marina about what had happened, she did not answer them.

"What happened when you took her into custody?" Jenna asked the first cop, who was named Officer Ryan.

"I interrogated her," he said.

"And how did that go?" Jenna asked.

"Not good," Officer Ryan said. "She didn't answer our questions properly at all."

"What do you mean that she wasn't answering your questions properly?"

"I mean, she gave nonsense answers. For instance, I asked her about what she was doing in her house at the moment her husband died, and she started talking about what happened when she was seven years old. She talked about going to the zoo with her adoptive mother, and I asked her if she killed him and she started talking about sea lions. It was weird."

And he went on to tell the jury about the rest of the interrogation.

I knew this testimony was not exactly good testimony for Jenna, but I also knew she would be calling an expert who could testify about dissociative states, and how individuals can commit murder while they're in that state. That was important for her to show. Because, if my client really was catatonic at the time the cops had come to the scene, how could she have killed him? So that expert was next.

The prosecutor's expert witness was named Dr. Little. She was a slight blonde woman, about 45 years old, who wore glasses, put on no makeup, and had kind of a mousy look to her. She walked slightly stooped and was a tiny person, living up her name. She probably only weighed about 90 pounds.

She gave her name on the stand, and her credentials,

stating to the jury that she had been a psychotherapist for the past twenty years and had earned her PhD from Harvard in clinical psychology. She stated that she had treated a multitude of patients over the years who had dissociative states, including people who had suffered from Dissociative Identity Disorder, explaining to the jury that DID had been commonly known as Multiple Personality Disorder, and patients who dissociated because they were suffering from another mental illness, such as Borderline Personality Disorder.

"Can you explain to the jury what a dissociative state is?" Jenna asked her.

"It's basically where an individual has, what sometimes is been termed, an out-of-body experience. Some patients have described it as seeing themselves from up above, or from another room, and not feeling that they're a part of their own body."

"So some patients describe it as not being part of their own body?"

"Yes. It's a detachment from reality. It can be distinguished from a loss of reality which is the case in psychosis. Dissociation is the way a patient copes when he or she is experiencing a period of extreme stress. It could be mild, such as daydreaming and getting yourself lost in your daydreams. Most people have experienced that kind of mild dissociation, where they have a daydream which seems very real, but it's not. But it can also manifest itself as an altered state of consciousness."

"And what do you mean by altered state of consciousness?" Jenna asked Dr. little.

"Well it could mean different things. It could mean the person thinks the world is unreal. She's not a part of that the world and she's not a part of herself. It could mean a loss of memory, amnesia. Sometimes a person forgets who they are, and assumes a new identity, a new sense of self. It can also manifest with Dissociative Identity Disorder, commonly known as multiple personality disorder, where there's different personalities within the same body. It could manifest itself as post-traumatic stress disorder, where an individual is brought back to a time of extreme stress, and relives that moment over and over, in minute detail."

"What brings on dissociative states?" Jenna asked.

"Stress is commonly what triggers dissociative states. Also trauma. Sometimes it's brought on by the person taking psychoactive drugs. But sometimes it doesn't have a trigger."

"And what causes dissociation, at its root?"

"Usually trauma. Dissociation helps a child, or an adult, who's in an abusive situation, survive his or her situation. For instance, if a person is being abused, a person may dissociate because he or she needs to escape that reality. Literally. It's a defense mechanism, so even after the traumatic situations have ended, the brain still remembers the trauma, so the dissociation can happen for years afterwards."

"And, to your knowledge, is it possible to kill another person while you're in a dissociative state?"

"Yes. It definitely is."

And then she explained about a number of public cases she had studied throughout the years where people had killed individuals while they were in such a state. She gave several examples where people had multiple personalities and one of the personalities killed somebody. This was not considered to be an excuse for the murder. But she also talked about how individuals who did not have DID were shown to have killed somebody while they were in a dissociative state. They would not remember the murder afterwards, and, as a matter of fact, they were in this dissociative state when they killed the individual.

Her testimony lasted several hours, and then, finally, Jenna announced she was through with her direct examination of Dr. Little. "I have nothing further for this witness," Jenna said, and then sat down.

I approached Dr. Little. "Dr. Little, is it fair to say that you have not actually treated my client?"

"Yes, that that is fair to say. I have not treated your client."

"In fact, you're just here to be a general expert witness, to state that it's possible to kill in a dissociative state, isn't that right?"

"Yes, that is correct."

"So you don't know for sure that my client actually killed her husband while she was dissociating, correct?"

"Right. That's correct. I have no idea if she did that."

"You talked on direct about all of these cases of people that you have heard about. People that you have read about in studies. Isn't that right?"

"Yes, that's correct. Those were all case studies. I obviously would not be able to testify about people I actually treated. That would be a clear breach of doctor-patient confidentiality."

I knew what she was getting at. She was implying that, even though she did not actually state on the stand that she treated people who killed somebody while dissociating, she actually did treat some patients like that but she could not state that on the stand. I would pin her down on that, because I knew for a fact that she did not have any patients who killed someone while in a dissociative state. This was something I discovered when I interviewed her myself.

"In fact, you have never actually treated a patient who killed another individual while they were dissociating, isn't that true?"

"Yes, that's true."

"So, are you telling the jury that your only knowledge of people killing other people while dissociating are through the case studies you have read and in medical journals which are available to the public. Isn't that right?"

"Yes, that's correct. But I have treated many patients who have had dissociative states throughout their lives."

"I understand that. You stated that when you first took the stand. You stated that you were a bit of an expert on dissociative states. I just wanted to pinpoint that you had not actually had a patient who killed in such a state. And that's your testimony, isn't that right?"

"Yes, as I said, that is correct."

"I have nothing further for this witness."

Dr. Little was excused and she left the stand.

I felt pretty good about my exchange with her. After all, she was supposed to be this big expert, but she wasn't that much of an expert, because she had never treated anybody who was in the same situation my client was in when her husband died.

I realized that Marina's dissociative state kind of boxed the prosecutor in and I was happy about that. She had to address it, and she had to explain it away. The jury still could not be sure that killing somebody while dissociating was actually a thing.

The next few witnesses were going to be more problematic. They were the ones who actually saw Marina and Lawrence interact.

The first witness the prosecutor called was named Ella O'Neill. Ella was one of Lawrence's oldest family friends.

She had known him since she was born. She was obviously not one of their sex site friends, so she did not feel embarrassed to take the stand. I knew the other ones were going to feel a sense of shame, but they were subpoenaed, so they couldn't really get out of it.

But Ella was a family friend. She was the daughter of Lawrence's best friend, whose name was Pete O'Neill. She had been to one dinner party where she was privy to all of what Marina could dish out to poor Lawrence.

Pete, her father, was also at the same dinner party, but he was in the hospital, so he could not testify. Ella, however could testify.

And testify she wanted to do.

Chapter Thirty-Five

ELLA APPROACHED THE WITNESS STAND, raised her right hand, was sworn in, and sat down. She glared at Marina. I could see hatred burning in her eyes. I looked over at Marina and she was glaring right back. Marina was not going to be intimidated by her or anybody else.

Ella burned a hole in Marina, a hole that I could tell was deep with hatred. Her eyes were turned on Marina, and they were accusing, scary. I could almost read what she was thinking in her head. She was thinking to herself, *you killed him, you know you did. He was a good man, and now he doesn't exist anymore just because of you.*

Perhaps she was right. I didn't really know. I had a good idea, however, that she was not correct that my client killed her husband.

She was sworn in, she stated her name, and then Jenna got right to work. "Now, Ms. O'Neill, you understand why you are testifying in court today, isn't that right?"

Ella got closer to the microphone. "Yes. I understand."

"Take me back to the evening of April 17 of last year.

Can you describe to me what you were doing that evening."

"Yes. I was a participant in a dinner party with myself, Lawrence, and his wife, Marina Vasiliev." She took a deep breath through her nose and blew it out her mouth. She closed her eyes, and I could tell that she was trying to find her happy place. I recognized that immediately because that was the kind of thing I did when I was nervous. Or scared. Or enraged. And I could tell this woman was suffering from that last emotion. Rage.

"And can you describe for the court what was the mood of that particular dinner party?" Jenna was now pacing around, looking at me and then looking over at the jury. She smiled at me a little bit, and I could tell she thought she had me on the ropes. And my client on the ropes as well. I just looked back at her, my eyes hopefully conveying that I would not be intimidated by her or anybody else. I stared at Jenna right back as she gave me a little smirk, and then turned back to Ella, who was still on the stand, still burning holes into Marina.

"It was tense, to say the very least." And then she looked over at Marina. "You ever seen the movie, or the play, *Who's Afraid of Virginia Woolf?* You know, where there's a married couple and they were just horrible to each other all through the night, right in front of two other people who had no idea what they were getting into? Hitting below the belt, right in front of their guests. Well that's what that night was like, only, in this case, it was only one of the parties hitting below the belt of the other. Marina kept hitting Lawrence, and he just took it."

"What do you mean, Marina kept hitting Lawrence, and he just took it?"

"What I mean is that Marina was constantly saying

horrible things to him all night long. Right in front of me. She was saying things about how he was in bed, telling him he was a terrible lover. She was saying things to him about how he could never satisfy her, either in bed or out. She was complaining about the fact that she was married to him and he had all his money, and why was she was only getting $1 million a year from him, because she knew he was worth billions. She told him she thought that he was running his company into the ground, and sooner or later, she wouldn't have anything to get from him. She said things like she wanted to make sure she got as much money as possible from him while she could, because she thought that by the time he was 70 years old, he would be worth nothing. Mind you, he was 60 years old when I was at the dinner party, so she was saying he would be broke in another 10 years. And she did not want to chance that she would get to the end of the marriage with him and have both of them broke and in the poorhouse."

At that, Marina was on her feet. "Of course I thought he would lose all his money. He was a terrible businessman, terrible CEO. I don't even know how he managed to get a business. And I grew up in an orphanage and –"

Judge Watt pounded her gavel and pointed right at marina. "Ms. Vasiliev, you need to sit down and be quiet. One more outburst like that and I will put you in contempt of court."

I stood up, and I put my hand firmly on Marina's shoulder. I could tell she was shaking with rage, and I could also tell that she wanted to go right over to Ella and strangle her. This was not a good look. Not a good look at all. The members of the jury were all looking at Marina and shaking their heads. I could tell they were not liking my client at this moment.

I could tell that Ella's testimony was affecting the jury, and I hoped I could overcome it. I didn't know if I could, however. I knew this was coming, and I knew Ella would be one of many who would testify as to how horrible Marina was to her husband. I knew Marina could not really help the way she was. When you have Borderline Personality Disorder, you really can't control your outbursts. Not that this was an excuse for the way she behaved - nothing could excuse that. She was not just cruel to Lawrence, but to everybody else around her, except maybe Amber, and, with her, I knew it was only a matter of time. At the same time, I also knew that, through my research on BPD, her behavior was pretty typical.

I was therefore happy that I had a therapist who would testify on her behalf. He would explain to the jury about BPD and tell them exactly why my client would act so horribly.

I just had to take a deep breath and listen to Ella's testimony and write down notes as fast as I could. I didn't really know what she would say, because I could not get a deposition from her because that's how it works in California. You cannot depose parties prior to a criminal trial, not unless the party wouldn't be available in trial. I personally thought that was a terrible rule, but that was the rule in California, so it was what it was.

"Okay, so you were privy to an exchange between Marina and Lawrence, where Marina was humiliating and hostile," Jenna said. "Is that right?"

"Yes, well, what can I say. This is not necessarily something out of the ordinary, from what I understood. Anyhow, that night, Lawrence was not saying a whole lot. I could tell, just by looking at him, that -"

I was on my feet. "Her answer is veering towards speculation, because it sounds like she's about to state what she thought Lawrence was thinking in his mind. And I would like to preclude that from happening. So, I would like for your honor to direct the witness not to state that she knows any kind of motivation in Lawrence's mind that night."

"Sustained." The judge looked at Ella. "Ms. O'Neil, please limit your testimony to actual words that you heard that night between Ms. Vasiliev and Mr. Murphy. And please do not try to speculate on what either party that night might've been thinking about the other. Please limit your testimony to the concrete evidence that you saw that night between the two of them as far as how they felt about each other."

Ella looked a bit confused, but I think she understood. "OK. Well, I can just tell you that Lawrence did not say much that night. Marina was doing all the talking. She was angry, judging by her words to him. And I don't really know exactly why she was angry. I just know she was."

"And what did she say to him, besides what you testified to earlier?"

"She said she wished he were dead. She said that several times. I wish you were dead. I wish you were dead. I must've heard that at least five times that night."

"And what were you doing while all this was happening?" Jenna asked.

"Wishing I was someplace else. Wishing the floor would open up and swallow me whole. I had no idea that I would be getting into such a viper's nest. Lawrence is a good friend of mine. He was my father's partner from way back when. I've known him since I was a little girl. And I've been away for a number of years, living on the East Coast, so I had not seen him in a while. I was anxious to see him that night. So that's why I decided not to leave. In fact, I thought he probably would want my company because Marina was treating him so terribly all through the night. Otherwise, I probably would've begged off. I probably would've said I had something to do, a headache, anything to get away from there. But I stayed. And now, I'm kind of glad I did, because I can now testify in court exactly what I saw that night. What I heard that night."

I would have a tough time cross examining this woman. Marina told me what she would say, and, apparently, everything she was saying about what Marina said to Lawrence was 100% correct. I didn't know that Marina hated her husband so much, and I really didn't know why.

I mean, I knew why she hated him now. I just had no clue exactly why she hated him back then. Except for the fact that, obviously, the demon came out that night. The demon that Marina just cannot control.

"OK, so you witnessed her telling Lawrence several times that she wished he were dead. Did you hear any kind of threats from her to him?"

"Yes. I did. I heard her say to him several times, 'just don't forget that I have a gun.' She said that twice. I have to admit, I was extremely frightened about her saying that to him. And then he finally had enough. He talked about taking that gun away from her."

I knew that was not hearsay because that particular comment was not being used to prove the truth of the matter asserted. It was being used as proof that Lawrence did not want the gun in the house, and that Lawrence would try to take it away from her, but it did not prove that she actually used that gun.

Nevertheless, I decided to object for the record, which was the way you preserved objections for any further appeals. "Objection, hearsay," I said, getting into my feet.

"Overruled." Judge looked at the witness, and nodded her head. "You may proceed."

"Yes, he finally stood up for himself. He finally had enough. He told her that he would get that gun away from her, and she said back to him that he couldn't get it away from her, because he didn't know where it was. She had hid it. And then she started talking to him about all the lovers she was taking, most of them female. Which was weird, I thought. By this time, Lawrence had sat back down, and he wasn't looking at either me or Marina. I felt sorry for him and I knew I would have to talk to him later about what he was going through."

"So are there any other statements you heard from Marina to Lawrence that night?"

"Well, at some point, she seemed to have calm down. Just all at once, it seemed like she was a different person. It was the strangest thing. It's like she didn't even know the other person existed. The other person who was screaming, yelling, threatening, accusing and saying those horrible things just disappeared. It was like a switch was flipped and she was nice as pie. In fact, she asked me if I wanted some pie. I didn't want any pie, because what I saw at that dinner party earlier made me sick to my stomach. I just could not understand why the good man I grew up with, the man that was like a second father to me, why he would put up with such abuse. And that's what it was, abuse. That's the only word I can use to describe it. It was verbal abuse, and she was threatening him with a lot more than that."

"So what did you think in your mind when you found out Lawrence was murdered?"

"What do you think I was thinking? Obviously, the first thing I thought was that Marina did it. Then I read in the papers that she was arrested for his murder and I wasn't at all surprised."

I looked over in Marina and she was studying her nails. Then she looked at me and smiled. I didn't know if that smile was the smile that told me she would find this woman after the trial and strangle her, or it was a smile that told me that the good Marina was back, sitting next to me, patiently listening to this woman and not reacting.

Either scenario would not have surprised me at this point.

I knew I would have to cross-examine her, and cross-examine her hard. She had done a lot of damage to Marina. I knew that by looking at the jury. They were staring at Marina and they had as much hatred in their eyes as Ella. It didn't help that Marina was looking at the jury with a smug smile on her face. Again, I could not tell what that smile meant. Was that smile a sign of the bad Marina thinking *yeah, I did it. What are you going to do about it?* Or if it was a sign of the good Marina, trying to persuade the jury that she was not that kind of a person? She was not the kind of person who would attack her husband in front of a long-time friend, at a dinner party, and make Elizabeth Taylor in *Who's Afraid of Virgina Woolf* look like not a wolf, but a pussycat?

Again, I didn't know the answer to that question. I only knew I had work to do and I had to do it quickly.

Chapter Thirty-Six

JENNA ENDED her direct exam of Ella, and it was time for my cross.

"Ms. Neil, you stated on direct that you watched an abusive conversation between my client and her husband, Lawrence. Is that correct?"

"That's correct. Obviously that's what I was saying on direct. I don't really understand why you're asking me this question."

"Ms. O'Neill, I will ask the questions, and I would ask that you not interject. Now you also stated on direct that you heard my client talking to Lawrence, in a stern voice, telling him, among other things, that she wanted him dead.

"That was my testimony."

"Now you also heard her talk about the fact that she had a gun and Lawrence finally had enough and stated that he would take that gun away from her. Did you go to law enforcement about this?"

"No. I did not."

"But you stated on direct that you were concerned about his well-being, correct?"

"Yes. That's what I said. And that's what I meant. I was very concerned for his well-being."

"But you were not concerned enough to actually tell anybody in law enforcement about this, isn't that right?"

"That's correct."

"Why did you not go to law enforcement after you witnessed my client threatening her husband, your good friend?"

"Because I thought it was just a fight between a husband and wife. Or, rather, a wife verbally attacking her husband. As I said, Lawrence didn't fight back, except for when she was talking about that gun."

I went over to the jury and looked right at them as I asked her the next question. "OK, so your testimony is that you did not go to law enforcement because you were just watching a squabble between a husband and wife. Because if you really thought my client would kill her husband, you would've gone to the police, wouldn't you have?"

"Not necessarily. I mean, I had no proof she would do something to him."

"You didn't think she would do anything to him?" I asked in a voice that said I couldn't believe what I was hearing. "She was talking about a gun, she was talking about how she wanted him dead, and you didn't feel it was appropriate to go to the police and tell them you thought Lawrence was in danger?"

"No. I thought it was just words."

"Oh, so you thought it was just words. Are you telling the court that you thought you were just witnessing idle words?"

I was doing what I knew people hated about defense

attorneys. I was taking her testimony and deliberately misconstruing it. I knew what she meant. I knew that she probably didn't go to law enforcement because nobody would in that position. Most people in that situation would just watch people like that and automatically think they were just blowing off steam. You only realize later on that, when one of the people ended up dead, you were watching something much more serious. Yet I would make the fact that she did not go to the police an important part of my counter-narrative.

"Right, I thought they were just hurtful words."

"You thought they were just words. Just words. You didn't believe Lawrence was in danger that night, did you?"

"Well, I thought he might be. I mean-"

"No, you did not think he was in danger that night. If you would've thought that, you would've called the police."

Ella took a deep breath. She looked over at Marina and then at me. The hatred burning in her eyes was now directed at me and I welcomed that. It meant I was getting to her.

She was quiet for second. She knew she was defeated, and I knew I had drawn blood. That's what I wanted to do.

I had to neutralize this person, because if I didn't, the jury would decide that it was all she wrote. They were going to decide that my client killed her husband, even before I was able to put my evidence on.

"I should've gone to the police. I should've told the police that Marina had a gun and that she would use it on her husband. I guess maybe if I would've done that, he would still be alive. I guess it's my fault that Lawrence is dead. I guess that's what you're saying, isn't it?"

"No. I'm simply stating that your testimony on direct made it sound as if you really were concerned about

Lawrence's well-being that night. All I'm saying is that it's not accurate that you were genuinely concerned about his well-being, otherwise you would've done something about it. That's the only thing I'm trying to say."

I cross-examined her for another twenty minutes, and then I sat down.

I looked over at Marina, who was still smiling that enigmatic smile. I had no idea what she was grinning about, but maybe she was just going to her happy place.

Jenna put on other witnesses who were along the same vein as Ella. Through witness after witness, the nature of Marina's relationship with Lawrence was clear. He was cowardly, submissive to his wife. He took her abuse and didn't seem to fight back. Granted, I knew exactly why he was taking her abuse. I knew why he was not fighting back.

It was because he knew something she didn't. All those years, he knew the reason why he was with her.

It was guilt. Plain and simple. Guilt.

That was why he put up with her. Because he felt partially responsible for how she was. It was why he took her abuse and did not fight back. It was why he spent most of his life trying to get her help through one therapist after another.

He wanted to save her.

Because he knew he was partially responsible for breaking her in the first place.

It was why he learned everything he could about Borderline Personality Disorder, and what caused it.

After all, he knew what Dr. Weber had done. He understood it and he commissioned it. Dr. Weber worked for him and he was the CEO. He was responsible for what his company did.

Did Lawrence always know what Dr. Weber was doing?

No. I figured that out by looking at the emails between the two men. I knew that when Dr. Weber was doing what he was doing, Lawrence had no clue about it.

I also knew one other thing.

For years and years, Lawrence had no clue that Marina and Oksana were not the only ones.

Chapter Thirty-Seven

THE PROSECUTOR'S case went on for another few days, as witness after witness testified about the relationship they saw between Marina and Lawrence. By the end of it, I knew we were in trouble. Nevertheless, I had to plug on. It was up to me to ensure that the jury knew the truth about what had happened

After three days of hell, the prosecutor finally rested, and it was my turn to put on evidence.

I really only had four material witnesses I wanted to call, and one expert witness. The first material witness was Marina herself. Then I would call Marina's doctor. Then I would call Brock.

And then I would call Dr. Weber. He would be my star witness. Because I had no doubt in my mind that he was responsible for killing Lawrence.

And I would prove it.

So, when it was finally time for me to call my witnesses, I called Marina first.

She would have to tell the jury exactly why she was

treating her husband that way. She would have to explain about her diagnosis, and how she could not control it. She had to convince the jury that she was just blowing off steam and she would never hurt her husband. And she would have to be convincing, because, right at that moment, the members of the jury were glaring at Marina as if she was the Anti-Christ.

I got on the stand, she was sworn in, she stated her name, and I got work. "Now, Ms. Vasiliev, do you understand why you're on the stand right now?"

She cocked her head at me, and I kind of knew she was not the devil. She was not Malphas or whatever she called her demon. I hoped and prayed she stayed that way. Then again, I knew the bad part of her could come out just anytime. I was afraid of that happening.

"Yes, I do understand why I'm here," she said with a nod of her head. "The prosecutor thinks I killed my husband. I have to admit that after hearing some of those witnesses, I don't blame the state of California for thinking that. I don't blame the jury for thinking that. I was awful to him."

"Well, before we get into that, I'm going to ask you a few other questions. Can you tell me a little bit about your background, about your early childhood?"

Jenna was on her feet. "Objection, I don't see how this is relevant."

I rolled my eyes. "Obviously, it's relevant. Her background will explain why she has a personality disorder that she can't control, and in return, will also explain exactly why she treated her husband the way she did."

There was one other witness I would call - an expert witness about BPD. I needed the therapist to testify about her treatment and how borderlines feel about themselves.

How they project the hatred for themselves on other people. That was the main thing I needed the court to know - the hatred that Marina had projected upon Lawrence was actually hatred of herself.

"Objection overruled," Judge Watts said. "Miss Vasiliev, you may answer the question."

Marina looked unsure of herself. "I was born in the old Soviet Union. Leningrad, now known as St. Petersburg. I was orphaned at a very young age. Or at least I thought I was orphaned at a young age."

I told her about her mother several months ago. When she found out about Olga, Marina refused to see her. She could not bear the thought that her mother had sold her. She told me that a part of her understood her mother doing what she did. She understood that her mother thought she could not take care of her and Oksana and that they would all die of starvation if she didn't do something. But the thing that really pissed her off was that her mother got so much money for her and that she came to America. She was also furious that her mother didn't care enough about her to make sure she found a good home. Her mother should have questioned Dr. Weber more, and she should have insisted that she meet both adoptive families for her and Oksana. Or, even better, Olga should have insisted that she and Oksana stay together. Olga should have done something, anything, to make sure Marina was not left at an orphanage.

The upshot was that she and Olga never did reconcile.

"Can you tell the court what you mean when you said you thought you were an orphan?"

"Yes. That's what I was always told by the ladies of the orphanage. That's what I was told by Svetlana Kazakova. She was the main person I dealt with when I was a young child, desperate for a home. I was only three months old when I was brought there. When I got to be a little older, and I could understand about the world a little bit more, I used to ask about why I was there, because I knew other children had parents, and I did not. When I was very little, I did not even know the concept of parents. But I learned it. I learned it by going out in the world and seeing some of the other kids."

"What do you mean that you learned it by going out in the world and seeing it with other kids?"

"The ladies of the orphanage would take us out. You know, we would go out to McDonald's, places like that. We went out to different shopping places around Leningrad, field trips, things like that, when I was very young. I would see kids with a man and a woman. I'll admit, I didn't really understand who these people were around these children. So I asked Mrs. Kazakova about that, about the men and the women who were around kids, and how come I didn't have those same men and woman around me. She wouldn't answer my question. But later on, when I went to school, I saw my classmates had that same thing. A man and woman with them. I was starting to understand that other kids had parents. It just dawned on me that I was living in a place where I didn't have that. I learned when I was six years old what had happened to my parents. I was told they were both killed in a car accident."

"Did you understand, at that time, that you were living in an orphanage?"

"By then, yes I did. I understood what an orphanage was. I understood the other kids who were with me didn't have parents either."

She proceeded to tell the jury about what had happened to her in the orphanage. She explained to them about how when she was a small child, a baby, she came to realize that she had been touched inappropriately by men around her.

"At the time, I didn't know what was happening, but it was something has always stuck with me, all of my life. When I was not even one year old, there was a man, I don't know who it was, who put his finger up inside of me. I remember it, because I felt even then that there was something wrong."

"Did you ever find out who that man was?" I asked her.

"I did. I found out his name was Sergei Dmitriev. He was somebody who worked at the orphanage. I think he was somebody who cleaned up after us, or something like that. I also remembered that, throughout my early childhood, he would do things to me. I didn't know it was wrong at the time."

She told the jury about how Sergei had touched her genitals throughout her early childhood. She told the jury that he not only his put his fingers there, but also his mouth.

And then she told the jury about what happened next. "Beginning when I was six years old, he raped me. He raped me a lot." She looked down at the stand and then back up at me.

Then, I saw it. She looked at me but I could tell she was not there anymore.

She was dissociating, even as I looked at her.

I tried to ask her some questions, but she would not answer. She just stared straight ahead, looking at nothing. I wondered if she would be okay in just a few minutes. I knew that, after talking to her therapist, and through talking to her, the dissociation sometimes would last only few minutes and sometimes for several days. It usually happened when she was having to bring up the painful memories of her early childhood.

"Mr. Vasiliev," Judge was saying to her. "Could you please answer the question?"

And, just like that, she was back. "I'm so sorry. What was the question?"

"I was just asking you when you were able to get out of the orphanage?"

"I left the orphanage when I was seven years old. I found an adoptive family. The Williams. They adopted me and brought me here in San Diego. I lived the rest of my life here. They were good, kind, and loving, but I couldn't get over what happened to me back in the orphanage. I couldn't get over the rapes, the molestations, the neglect, the abuse. I couldn't get over the days I didn't eat, the days I was chained to a bed and made to lie in my own filth. I had dirty diapers for days and days. I remembered all of it. I couldn't get over laying in a bed in the dead of winter, no blankets, dark, nobody to hear me cry. I could never get over knowing that I was alone in the world and there was nobody there for me. I was broken and there was just no way that anybody would be able to put me back together."

I glanced over at the jury and saw that several of them had tears in their eyes. They were watching Marina, transfixed by her story.

"Now is it your understanding that you have been diagnosed with a certain personality disorder?"

"Yes."

"What is that personality disorder?"

"Borderline personality disorder."

"So, let's get back to your relationship with your husband, Lawrence. You heard the testimony of the other witnesses. They talked about how you humiliated Lawrence, how you told him constantly how you hated him, how you told him that you wished he was dead. Did you really feel that way?"

"No. I did not feel that way."

"How did you feel about your husband?"

"Grateful. I knew he was a good man and I was grateful he took me in. Although my adoptive parents were loving, I knew they probably did not want me to live with them for the rest of their lives. And I didn't have any kind of skills or good education, so I was happy Lawrence gave me a good home."

"When you say that you're grateful for Lawrence giving you a good home, do you mean that you loved him, like a husband?"

"No. I didn't love him like a husband. I saw him more as somebody who was taking care of me. And he did. He took care of me financially and by giving me a roof over my head. He gave me everything I needed to live. So, yes, I was grateful to him."

"Yet the witnesses talked about how cruel you were to him. Can you explain that?"

She nodded. "I can explain it. I've had so much therapy over this, you would not imagine. But what I have come to know is that I hate myself. I've always hated myself. I loathe who I am. I look at myself sometimes and feel sick. And, because Lawrence was around, he was the person who I was projecting my own hatred, my own self-loathing, onto. When I told him I wished he was dead, I was really saying I wished I was dead. When I told him I hated him, I was really saying I hated myself. When I told him I thought he was ugly, it was because I'm ugly. When I would tell him that I wished he was never born, it was because I felt that about myself. Everything I said to him were things I was thinking about myself."

"So you actually didn't hate him, wish that he was never born, and wanted him dead?"

"No. Never. I never thought bad things about him. I wish that I could've controlled what I said to him in front of other people. That's another thing I found out about my illness. Sometimes, a certain thing takes over. I call it my demon. She takes over, and when she starts going, I can't control her. I can't control the things that come out of my mouth. But no, I never wanted him dead. I wanted myself dead. When I was talking about coming after him with a gun, I was wanting to use that gun on myself. I never wanted to kill him. He was a good man. And I would have never done it. "

"Okay. Now. Did you recently find out something that surprised you?"

"Yes. I did. I found out I have an identical twin sister."

"When did you find that out?"

"I found that out about eight months ago."

"How did you find out about her?"

"I found her because she called me. Actually she is now a he. Her name was Oksana when she was born. Now it's Brock, because she's now a boy. So, I'm going to try to refer to my sister as he from now on. Anyhow, he called me. He said that he saw me on the Internet. He came across my picture. I don't know, I think there was a picture taken of me and Lawrence, we were at some kind of a fund raising function. And Brock said he saw that picture of me and he saw himself. He knew what he looked like before he got into a lot of drugs and he started taking male hormones.

Anyway, he just had a feeling, all of his life, that there was somebody else who was supposed to be with him. Just like I've always felt like there was somebody out there who was my other half. And even though his adoptive parents had never told him he had a twin, he just always felt empty. Like he was only half there. I always felt the same way and I could never explain it either. So when he called me and said he felt like I was his long-lost twin, I didn't question him. In fact, it sounded right to me, more right than anything had ever sounded."

"So what happened next?"

"He gave his phone number and we talked. And it was odd, because I was talking to a boy, but at the same time, I just had a strong feeling that he was my long-lost sister. We agreed to meet."

"What happened when you met?"

"He came ready with a photo album. I guess because he thought that I would not believe him when I saw him. And, I had to admit, when I saw him, I did not see the resemblance at all. At the same time, I felt an unbelievable connection to him. Like I was finally finding the person who was my missing puzzle piece. Not in a romantic way, of course. But the missing link. I really felt a strong connection to him, so he didn't even have to show me those pictures. But he did show me the pictures anyhow. There were pictures of him when he was 20 years old and he was living with his parents before he was really into drugs and before he started taking the hormones. I saw those pictures were of me. I really believed him then."

"But yet, you kept his existence secret from your husband, right?"

"Yes. That's right. I mean, I wanted Lawrence to meet him. But I did not want him to know who he was. So, I asked him to open up a profile on ALT.com, the site that Lawrence and I used to find our partners, and he did. Then I contacted him over that site and pretended that was how he met me. I don't know, I just didn't want Lawrence to see him with me and ask me how I got to know him. So that's what I did."

"So he came over to visit with you guys?"

"Obviously, he was not going to actually be our sex partner. I mean, he was my identical twin sister, obviously I wasn't going to be doing anything sexual with him. I just told my husband that he was coming over to meet and greet and Lawrence was okay with that. Because we did that sometimes with people we met over the sex line. We didn't necessarily want to play, but we would have a meet and greet. That's how I introduced Lawrence to Oksana. I mean Brock."

"Now you said you didn't want Lawrence to know that you even had an identical twin sister. Why is that?"

"I don't know. I just kind of wanted to have something that was private from Lawrence. I don't know why I hid it. I just wanted to make sure I kept it from him."

"Now did you recently find out something about your husband?"

"Yes. I did."

"What did you find out about your husband?"

"I found out —" she began. And then she looked down at the witness stand and I could see she was shaking. She was near tears. "I found out he already knew I had an identical twin. He knew that because he was in on it."

"Now, you're saying to the jury that you found he was in on it. What do you mean by that?"

"I mean that I found out I was a part of an experiment that this Dr. Weber person was overseeing. When I discovered Dr. Weber did that, I was devastated. I was left in an orphanage, I lived through hell, all because this evil man, Dr. Weber, wanted it that way."

"And how did your husband factor into this?" I asked.

Another deep breath. "I found out that my husband knew about me. He specifically knew about my experiment, about what happened to me, and that was why he married me. He wanted to give me a good life, because he felt responsible for me going through all that when I was a small child."

"And how did you find this out?"

"I came across some emails he wrote to Dr. Weber where they discussed me."

I would go into detail about the emails, and I knew they would be admissible. I had prepared a pretrial motion for the admissibility of these e-mails and the judge had agreed with me. As long as Marina was able to lay a foundation for the emails, I could get them in. I would use Dr. Weber to authenticate the emails, because he was the sender and the recipient of these documents.

"Before you go any further, can you tell the court how you got ahold of these emails?"

"Yes. They were on my husband's computer. I did not alter them in any way, shape or form."

Jenna stood up. "I would like to object to the lack of foundation for these emails," she said.

I realized I had gotten ahead of myself. I needed Dr. Weber to authenticate them. "Your honor, may I approach?" I asked.

Judge Watts nodded and motioned Jenna and me to come to the bench. "Your honor, we discussed this in my motion *in limine*. We agreed that these emails would be admissible."

"Yes, but only if you can get them authenticated by Dr. Weber," Judge Watts said. "I think you need to call him to the stand and authenticate them before you can proceed."

I sighed. "Can we take a break and I can call him to the stand?"

"Yes," Judge Watts said. And then Jenna and I took our seats. "Ladies and gentlemen of the jury," Judge Watts announced, "I would like to take a 20-minute break so that counselors can authenticate some evidence. Don't stray very far, and please be back at 2:15."

I took a deep breath as the jury filed out. I didn't want Dr. Weber to have a heads-up on the email situation before I called him, but I knew there wasn't anything that could be done at this point. If the only way I would get these emails in was to get Dr. Weber on the stand to state that he was a part of the email chain, then I would just have to do it that way.

Dr. Weber came in the door after the bailiff found him. He looked confused as he approached the stand. "I don't know what's going on. Am I testifying now?" he asked, looking at the empty jury box.

"No, Dr. Weber, we just need for you to authenticate some documents before they're entered into evidence," Judge Watts said.

My heart was pounding. Dr. Weber took the stand and was sworn in. He stated his name for the record, and then I approached him.

"Dr. Weber, I would like for you to examine some emails that I have subpoenaed from Pegasus, Inc.," I said.

I handed him all the emails I printed out and he took out some reading glasses and read them. I saw his face go pale as he realized what was going on, and I silently kicked myself. He would know how I would attack him now. He would be prepared.

He handed them back to me, after reading them carefully for a good twenty minutes. I saw the jury was back.

They were outside the courtroom, looking in. *They were just going to have to wait a few minutes more.*

"Yes, I was the recipient of these emails," he said.

"And the words that have been printed on these emails are yours and Lawrence Murphy's, is that right?"

"Right."

"And these emails have not been altered in any way?"

"Right." I could see his wheels were turning in his head.

"I would like to enter these emails into evidence, your honor," I said.

Judge Watts nodded her head. "Ms. Powell, do you have any objections to these emails being admitted into evidence?"

She examined her copies of the emails, as if she had never seen them before. She had seen these emails before, of course, because I had given them to her months ago.

"No objection."

"These emails are entered into evidence," Judge Watts said. "Thank you very much, Dr. Weber," she said to him. "You are excused for now, although you will be re-called by the defense."

He looked furious by everything. He knew after seeing the emails that he was royally screwed. I just hoped that I could still take him by surprise when I called him.

Dr. Weber left, the jury came back in, and Marina was re-called to the stand. She was reminded that she was still under oath, and I approached her.

"Now, Ms. Vasiliev, before we took that recess, you were testifying about how you found out your husband knew about your situation at the orphanage, right?"

"Yes."

"And how did you find this out?"

"I saw some emails between Lawrence and Dr. Weber."

"And what did these emails say?"

"They talked about how Dr. Weber deliberately left me in an orphanage for the first seven years of life. I was a part of an experiment where Dr. Weber separated me from my twin, and made sure that Oksana had one kind of life and I had another very different life. I was deliberately left in a horrible situation and Oksana was placed in a good situation."

"So you found out your husband knew about this?"

"Yes he did. He found that out six years ago, which was when we got married."

"And how did you meet him?" I asked.

"He came into the coffee shop where I was working. I was working at Starbucks, and he came in and started talking to me. I thought he was a handsome guy. Charming. Intelligent. But I didn't think anything of it. Because obviously, I didn't think that somebody like him would be interested in someone like me."

"Why did you not think that he wouldn't be interested in you?"

"Well I found out he was extremely wealthy and I was a 24-year-old barista. And he was, you know, 50. But he pursued me. He asked me for my phone number and, about two months after we met, he asked me to marry him."

"Did you find out how he found you in the first place?"

"Yes. I discovered the truth about that through these emails."

"And how did he find you in the first place?"

"Apparently he had hired a private detective to find me. A private detective found me and told him I was working at Starbucks, and that I lived in San Diego, and that's when he decided that he would go out and meet me, specifically, and ask me to marry him. When he found out what had happened to me at the orphanage because of Dr. Weber, his employee, he decided to find me and give me the life I was missing when I was a little girl. He felt terribly guilty about what had happened to me. At least, that's what I gathered from the emails."

"So, Lawrence felt guilty about what had happened to you because of his company's experiment, so he decided to marry you and pay you a million a year to be married to him. Is that correct?"

"Yes. That's right. At least, that's what he told Dr. Weber."

"He found out about the two of you six years ago, and can you tell by the emails, exactly how he found this out?"

"Well, as I said, he's the CEO of the Pegasus company but he's not all that involved with the day-to-day operations. He's not a micromanager, so that's why he didn't know about this study in the first place. But then, I guess he was told about the study by a man by the name of Simon Thompson."

"Objection, hearsay," Jenna said, standing up.

"Your honor, the evidence regarding Simon Thompson goes to the notice that Lawrence had about my client's situation. His testimony does not go to whether or not Dr. Weber actually conducted this experiment, therefore it's not hearsay. And besides, my client is only testifying about what the emails state about Simon Thompson, and Dr. Weber has already authenticated these emails."

Judge Watts nodded. "I'll allow it. Please proceed, Ms. Vasiliev."

"Okay, now you were saying about Simon Thompson?"

"Right. Well, Simon was a guy working in the same division as Dr. Weber and was a whistleblower about my study. He specifically told Lawrence about what had happened with Oksana and me. And I guess that Lawrence did not fire Dr. Weber because Dr. Weber apparently threatened him and Dr. Weber said he believed Pegasus would be ruined if this got out. That was what I gathered when I reviewed the emails."

"And did your husband do anything about this study after Simon told him about it?"

"No. Aside from tracking me down and marrying me, he apparently didn't do anything. "

"I have nothing further for this witness," I said, sitting down.

I sat down, thinking I probably did all I could with her. I made her sympathetic and I showed the jury that she did not hate her husband, she hated herself.

Jenna knew she would have to treat Marina much more gingerly than she initially thought. But that was okay. She was able to finesse the situation and she delicately cross-examined her.

For the next hour and a half, Marina kept to her story even though Jenna crossed her as best she could. She was finally excused, and I was relieved.

We got through it.

Now, it was onto the good stuff.

Chapter Thirty-Eight

THE NEXT WITNESS I put on was Marina's doctor. Dr. Little took the stand to testify about Borderline Personality Disorder, what brings it on, what are the symptoms, and how the individual has a fractured sense of self. She explained to the jury that borderline makes the sufferers prone to rage, terrified of abandonment, and sufferers tend to have a shifting sense of self. They typically go from self-loathing to self-aggrandizement, and people are either bad or good to them.

She was able to explain Marina's illness well enough that I knew the jury knew that self-hatred was the cause of the borderline's rage and pain. She also explained that people with BPD are not any more violent than anybody else in the general population. That was very important that I got that out. I did not want the jury to think that because my client had this illness that she would be more violent than another person.

Brock was next on the the stand. He testified about how he found out that he, too, was a part of an experiment that he knew nothing about. His testimony was uneventful, but I just had to call him so the jury could get the other side of the story.

The next witness would be most important.

I would call Dr. Weber.

Chapter Thirty-Nine

DR. WEBER WAS NOT happy about being called. In fact, I had a hard time getting him to come to trial. I had to subpoena him, a subpoena that he had tried to quash several times. Of course - he knew what exactly happened. I guess he thought he would never have to answer for what he did.

Guess again.

I called him to the stand and he entered through the back doors, slowly walking towards the witness stand. His head was bent over and he looked furtively at the people in the gallery and at the members of the jury.

I hoped, if I did my job, that the jury would stop hating my client and start hating him. If things went well, this is exactly what would happen.

He raised his right hand and was sworn in, and I got to work.

"Could you please state your name for the record," I said.

"Dr. Robert Weber," he said, lifting his chin up slightly

in defiance. He was trying to convey that he wasn't intimidated, but then he meekly looked away and looked down at the witness stand.

"Can you explain to the jury how you are related to the victim in this case, Lawrence Murphy?"

"Yes. He's the CEO have Pegasus Inc., and I'm the head of the division that deals with twin studies."

"I see. And what do the twin studies entail?"

"Well, just what it says. I study twins. Identical twins. I am particularly interested in twins who have different environments. Like, if one twin was with one parent, and the other twin is with the other parent, in totally different environments. And I have done research studies on how different these twins are. How the environment affects each identical twin, and how it explains the diversions their behaviors, their personality and their intellect."

"I see. Now, do you study twins that have been separated at birth?"

"Yes, but that is very difficult to do."

"And why is that?"

"Because twins are not usually separated at birth. And when they are, they usually are adopted by families in a closed adoption. So I'm not able to get information about them."

"And did you find a way around that whole situation?"

"What do you mean?"

I looked at the judge. "Permission to treat as hostile," I said. I needed to treat this witness as a hostile witness so I could ask leading questions.

"Permission granted," the judge said.

"I mean, you found a way to study twins separated at birth," I said. "Twins who were put in completely different situations. You found a way to make sure that one twin was brought up in an abusive and neglectful situation and the other twin was given everything. Isn't that right?"

He looked over at the judge, over at the jury, and at me. He knew it was coming. He read the emails earlier. Yet he still looked like a cornered animal.

"Yes." He took a deep breath. "Yes. I did find a way around that whole situation."

"In fact, you managed to manipulate the situation by taking my client, Marina, and putting her into a Soviet orphanage and making sure she stayed there for the first seven years of her life, while her identical twin was adopted out by a very loving family, it isn't that right?"

"Yes."

"And, isn't it true that Lawrence found out about what you were doing, six years ago?"

"Yes. That's right."

I was pacing around. This was all stuff the jury had already known, because I brought it out in various ways, through Marina, through the emails, all of that.

But I would ask him the next four things the jury could not know about. "In fact, Marina and her identical twin Oksana, they were not the only children you did this with, isn't that right?"

Dr. Weber nervously scratched his forehead and then put his fingers to his hair. He looked down at the witness stand again, and he looked up at me and at the jury again. He looked like he wanted to find a way out the situation, any way he could possibly think of.

"Yes, that's right."

"In fact, you did this with 500 other kids, didn't you?"
"Yes."

Some of the jury members gasped and Judge Watts

glared at them. She motioned them to be quiet. I smiled when I heard the gasps because I knew I was winning.

"500 pairs of identical twins were separated at birth at your behest, right?"

"Right." He was still looking at the witness stand, his eyes not meeting mine. He was shaking. He knew he was caught.

"You went to developing countries that did not have very good records for their kids and you found as many identical twins as you could and you paid all these children's mothers to give up their children to you, isn't that right?"

"Yes. That's what I did. I would find a mother who would be struggling to care for her children, somebody who was desperate, and I would offer her a better life here in America, and money, if she would relinquish her children to me. Yes that's what I did."

He seemed almost proud of it now.

Maybe he was.

"You went to places all around the globe for this, didn't you?"

"Yes. That's what I did."

"In fact, you went to places like China, Thailand, Guatemala, El Salvador, multiple countries in Africa, the Philippines, any developing country, and you knew you could get away with it because there was lax enforcement with their adoption procedures. If you had difficulties getting these kids, you would just bribe the officials to get what you wanted. Isn't that right?"

"Yes. That's what I did. I don't think what I did was wrong. These mothers, they had no choice but to give their kids up. They certainly could not care for them. And in every one of these cases, one of the children got a life beyond what they could have ever dreamed of if I never came along."

"Fair enough. I guess I could say that if you were genuinely paying these mothers for their children, and you actually made sure both children were adopted, together, to a loving family, I would say you were not a monster. But that wasn't the case, now was it?"

"No. It was not the case."

"In fact, with all these kids, you did the exact same thing. Exactly what happened to my client, you did the same thing with all these 500 other pairs of kids. You gave one of the kids to an adoptive family. These families were clueless, for the most part, that there was another kid involved. But you made sure one of the kids was adopted through the proper adoption agency, and you made sure that kid was placed with a good family. The other kid, he or she wasn't so lucky, right? These kids were forced to stay in an orphanage for seven years. You made sure nobody could adopt them from the orphanage for the first seven years of their lives. Isn't that right?"

By now, he didn't even try to pretend he was anything but what he was – a monster.

"That's right. Listen, I had a very pinpointed study."

"What do you mean by pinpointed study?"

"My pinpointed study was to show how wildly divergent environments can affect identical twins. And, yes, I wanted to make sure the two twins had extremely divergent backgrounds. It wasn't enough that I studied two twins who lived with two different parents, one twin to the mother and one to the father, because usually in these cases, the father and the mother were roughly equal. Roughly equal socioeconomic status, roughly equal environments, roughly equal in every way. I mean, the mother might have less money than the father or the father might be more strict, or there might be other slightly divergent factors between the households. But the two households usually were too similar for me to determine, with any degree of certainty, how much nurture plays in a person's development. Plus, I had a very limited amount of material I could work with in studying these separated twins, because judges don't usually want to split up twins, so they usually don't award one twin to the mother and one to the father. So, yes, I had to manipulate the situation. I won't apologize for it. My research has yielded some really solid results. So yes, I had to go the extra mile to make sure I separated the twins myself, and that the environments could not be more different."

"I see," I said. "So you ruined the life of one of the kids, and, in every one of the situations you manipulated, I can assure you that one of the kid's life was ruined. I've spoken with some of the other twins and I can tell you they went through just much hell as my client did in their young lives. Those orphanages were not places where anybody should grow up in. Orphanages in poor countries are poorly funded, so these kids grow up in horrible conditions. Abuse, neglect, starvation. And you made sure each one of these 500 kids had to stay in the orphanage. If someone wanted to adopt them, they could not. You paid off every one of these orphanages to make sure that happened. These orphanages were so desperate for funding, they happily took your money and accepted your conditions. You did this for every child. Isn't that right?"

"That's right."

"And why did you do this study?"

"I had to do this study for our cloning division. Our company is on the cutting edge of human cloning, and we are working towards being the first company who will actually produce a human being through cloning. It's up to me to tell the parents who want to clone their kid how the kid's environment will shape them. So, it's very important this study was done."

"And isn't it true that Lawrence found out, within the past few months, exactly what you were doing with all these kids?"

Dr. Weber looked like he wanted to think about whether he wanted to lie or not. If he did try to lie, I would present him with the email chain, because that was how I found out about all of this. Marina showed me the email chain, and then I did my own research on all the kids he separated all over the world. Regina and I managed to track each one of them down, and I was able to talk to most of them. Most of them told me the same kind of war stories Marina told me. They all told me about the neglect and the abuse. Most of them had severe psychological effects from it, just like Marina had.

The kids who were adopted out when they were very young fared much better, unlike Oksana, but I was able to work with the adoption agencies who had adopted out them out and reunite them with their long-lost twin. Most of them were happy to find their twin, but they were also extremely enraged this happened.

"Yes. Lawrence found out about it."

"Actually, Lawrence knew about Marina years ago, didn't he?"

"Yes. He knew because a guy named Simon told him about it. He only found out about Marina, though, so Lawrence also only knew about Marina at that point."

"But he just recently found out you were doing it with a lot of other kids, didn't he?"

"Yes. He found that out."

"How did he find that out?

"He found it out from a different person. She was someone whom I trusted. I never trusted anybody with my study. I never told anybody about it, either. I wanted the study to be very controlled. But I met a woman. Edison Caldwell. I fell in love with her. I trusted her so I told her what I'd been doing with this kids. And she betrayed me. I was blindsided."

"Betrayed you. What do you mean by that?"

"She told Lawrence about the kids. She told him about the 500 kids I separated over the years."

"You mean 500 pairs you separated over the years, don't you?"

"Yes. That's what I mean. The 500 pairs I separated over the years. She found out about it and told Lawrence."

"She told Lawrence about it. What did he do?"

"He told me he would immediately go to the FBI and tell them what I did. He was going to consult with some attorneys about what would happen to his company if this got out. He had to do some succession planning and had to make sure the company did not completely go under when the lawsuits started. So I knew it was just a matter time before I was exposed."

"I see. So he was going to expose you, right?"

"Right. He was going to expose me."

"And you knew that if Lawrence went to the FBI, you would spend the rest of your life in prison, didn't you?"

He shook his head. "I don't know what I did wrong. I gave their mothers a better life. I gave one of the kids a better life. If I never stepped in, both the mother and both of the kids would have ended up dying in poverty. That is if both of the twins didn't end up in the orphanage anyway. What I did was give the mother and one of the kids a good life. I gave two of them a chance. If not for me, none of them would have had a chance."

He made a point, but I had to ignore it. "You were trafficking. You were buying children. That is against the law. Not to mention the fact that because one of the kids were kept in a terrible condition, you would be personally sued. You had a lot to lose, didn't you?"

"Yes, I had a lot to lose."

"You knew Lawrence knew about these kids, but, to your knowledge, nobody else did, isn't that right?"

He bowed his head. "Right."

"Not even Edison. Because she died, too, didn't she? She was killed by a mugger on the street right after she talked to Lawrence, wasn't she?"

I knew Dr. Weber was behind her death, too, but that wasn't a part of this trial, so I didn't want to bring that in.

"Yes, that's correct. The situation was kept between Lawrence and me. In fact, it was my understanding he never got a chance to even talk to attorneys exactly about what I did. He just wanted to make sure the company would be financially solvent when the lawsuits started coming."

"And you killed him to keep your secret, didn't you?"

He bit his lower lip. I wouldn't have been surprised if he admitted to that as well. That guy had a way of justifying absolutely anything in his head. He would probably tell the jury that killing Lawrence was the right thing to do, because, in his head, it was.

He lifted his chin and then looked at the jury. "Yes. I did."

And then he looked down at the witness stand again.

"Yes. You killed Lawrence?"

"Yes. I did," he repeated. "I did. I had to. He was going

to ruin me. I would be sued by all 500 of those kids, not to mention by their identical twin, the one who was placed in a good home, because I violated every ethical rule in the book. I would spend the rest of my life in prison. I panicked."

"I have nothing further for this witness," I said.

"I did nothing wrong," he mumbled. "I did nothing wrong. Those mothers, those kids, they all would have died if I didn't come along. What did I do wrong? I collected great data. No other study could come close to finding out the data I found out. Researchers have been studying the nature verses nurture question for years, and I've definitively answered it. What did I do wrong?"

He kept babbling like that while the bailiffs approached him and slapped the handcuffs on.

He kept babbling as they took him out of the courtroom.

He probably kept babbling all the way to the jail. I didn't know that for sure, but I imagined that, by the time they got him to the jail, they would be ready to kill him themselves just to shut him up.

After he left, Jenna stood up. "Well, I guess I need to dismiss this case with prejudice."

"I don't think you have a choice, Ms. Powell," Judge Watts said. "Ms. Vasiliev, you are free to go."

I looked over at her and smiled.

My very first at-bat, and I hit it out of the park.

Avery would be so proud.

Chapter Forty

THAT NIGHT, Regina and I were sitting on the beach. It was a dark, cool night, and we were sitting on a large blanket, just listening to the waves coming in.

Even though alcohol wasn't allowed, we didn't care. We each had a plastic wine glass filled with Chablis. For the moment, we weren't talking.

Regina looked over at me. "Aidan, I-"

I watched her, waiting for her to say something else.

But she didn't.

She just kissed me.

And I lost my breath.

Next in the Southern California Legal Thrillers Series

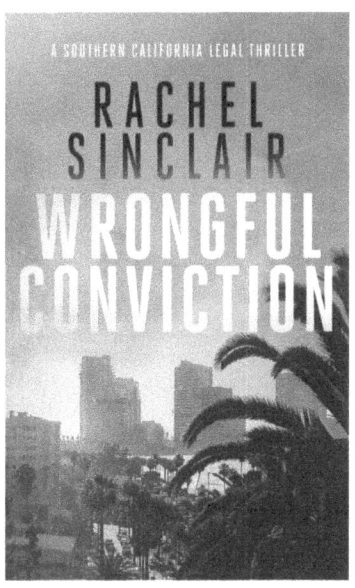

vinci-books.com/wrongful-conviction

A corrupt system. A powerful enemy. A lawyer's battle to free an innocent man.

Christian Davies has taken on a high-profile case for Jamel Jackson, a sixteen-year-old African American boy. He has been sentenced to life in prison for the vicious assault of a famous actress. As Christian delves into the trial court transcript, he uncovers a shocking truth: the real culprit is a well-connected and influential individual who will go to any lengths to keep Jamel locked away.

Turn the page for a free preview…

Wrongful Conviction: Chapter One

CHRISTIAN

I JUST GOT A NEW CASE – Jamel Jackson. I felt privileged to be representing him, because I had read about his case in the paper, and I couldn't help but think that he was getting a raw deal. He had been convicted of raping an actress. Not just any actress, but an A-list actress by the name of Felicity McDaniel. I had been following the case along and I just had a feeling there was something missing in the entire procedure.

So, when I went to see him in the jail, unannounced, I talked to him to get a sense as to what happened. The kid was just 18 and had been convicted for the rape of Ms. McDaniel, and to say he was frightened would be an understatement.

"Why are you here to see me?" he asked me. He was a slight African-American boy, only about 5'6" and probably a buck thirty, with braided hair, *café au lait* skin and fine features. He had obviously been crying, as his big brown eyes were bloodshot and red. "They just put me in jail. I'm going be serving life in prison. I don't have the money to pay nobody for an appeal, if that's what you're thinking."

He looked down at his hands, which were shackled, as were his legs. I knew he was due to be transferred to the state penitentiary, in Victorville, California, within days. From the looks of him, the prospect of going to a maximum security prison was terrifying for him. As it would be for anybody in his shoes.

I had a strong feeling this was an innocent boy looking back at me, and I knew nobody was going take his case. It was not only the fact that he had no money, but also because this was a case nobody wanted to touch with a 10 foot pole. Still, his situation did not deter me. Once I had a feeling an injustice was done, that's all I really knew.

"Listen, you only need to know one thing," I said. "And that's that I'm interested in your case. I don't even expect you to pay me. I know you don't have the money."

Jamel looked at me suspiciously. "Yeah, dog, don't nobody do nothing for free. Why do I think this will cost me more than cash?"

I folded my hands in front of me and looked at him silently. I was studying him, just as he was studying me. What I didn't really want to tell him was that I was very interested in this case because I just had a feeling the person who really raped Felicity was somebody who really needed go down, and hard. There was a shadowy figure behind his entire case, and I just had a feeling it was somebody who deserved justice. I wanted to be the one to give it to him.

What I knew about this case was that there was no DNA found inside of Felicity. She, herself, had no recollection of what had happened to her - she was beaten that badly. She'd been in the hospital for several months before she was even able to talk to the cops. She had severe memory loss and her abdomen had been kicked so viciously that she was bleeding internally. These were just her internal injuries. Externally, she had been savagely kicked, so she was bruised everywhere. Her eyes were swollen shut and it took the best plastic surgeon in Los Angeles to bring her to where she looked like herself again.

The best I could tell, the reason why this poor guy was in jail, and convicted, was because he was at the wrong place at the wrong time. He had explained to the court that he was an Uber delivery driver and Felicity apparently had ordered a sub sandwich from Subway to have delivered to her house. However, by the time he got there, according to what his court testimony was, he'd found she was not answering the door. He didn't know what to do, because he was new on the job, and didn't realize that in cases where the person doesn't answer the door, you're supposed to indicate on the app that nobody was answering, and then you have to wait a certain amount of time. If the person doesn't answer the phone or the door within that window of time, you can leave the food at the door and take a picture of it.

However, as Jamel had explained in his testimony, he wasn't aware of that provision. He thought he had to make every effort to deliver the food. So he'd gone around to the pool area to see if he could find her, and, he told the court, he found her laying by the pool, unconscious. He called 911 and they came to take her to the hospital. She almost died.

Of course, the prosecutor made hay about the fact that he was able to get into the pool area in the first place. After all, the pool area of her house was locked with a combination lock. The assumption was that if he was telling the truth, and he really was an Uber driver, and he just wanted to deliver her food, come hell or high water, he would not have been able to get back there.

Insanity Defense

This was one of the first errors I found in the case. His defense attorney did a terrible job. I knew that I would have to comb the transcripts for any kind of error the court made, but I knew that in the end, I would probably have to go with an ineffective assistance of counsel defense and try for a writ of *habeas corpus*. His defense attorney never even proposed the question of how would Jamel have been able to get back into the pool area even if he was the rapist. If the pool area was locked, it was locked. In fact, that was the entire hole in the entire case as far as I was concerned – there was no reasonable explanation as to how he could've gotten on the grounds in the first place. To me, the entire thing seemed to be a huge set-up.

I wasn't sure, but my instinct told me that what had happened was that the actual person who beat and raped her did so and then summoned an Uber delivery driver to come and deliver food, with the intention of eventually setting up the driver, whoever it was. The person who raped her deliberately left the pool area open and left the gate to her home open, and that person had taken the chance that the Uber driver would not have known that you're not supposed to go onto private property to deliver food. Indeed, I had reviewed the rules for Uber delivery drivers, and that's one of the things that they're not supposed to do – they are not supposed to go onto private property. If the person doesn't answer the door, the person doesn't answer the door. You leave the food at the door and go.

So the prosecutor was able to make hay about that entire thing as well. He was able to show that since it was Uber policy not to go onto private property, that meant Jamel's protestations that he was an innocent bystander were bullshit, because if he really was just an innocent

Uber driver, he would've followed the policy like he was supposed to.

Of course, if the defense attorney was doing his job, he would've hammered home the fact that Jamel was, indeed, delivering Uber at the time Felicity was found. That would have been easy enough to prove - all he would have to have done was subpoena the Uber dispatch to show that Jamel had indeed taken an order to Felicity's house and delivered it at that time. That would have bolstered Jamel's story. But the defense attorney didn't even bother to do that, so the prosecutor was able to successfully make the argument to the jury that Jamel wasn't delivering at that time, but that he had wandered in off the street, was able to scale the wall to Felicity's mansion and then scale the wall to her pool area, where he raped and beat her and then called 911.

None of it made sense to me. I knew Felicity's walls around her house and around her pool were made of stone and were 10 feet tall. The prosecutor was not able to really establish that Jamel would've been able to scale either one of those walls, let alone both of them, but again, the defense attorney did not question the theory that Jamel got onto the grounds by scaling the walls. In fact, the defense attorney did not even bother to go to the site and see exactly how high these walls really were.

There were so many errors committed by his attorney that I couldn't even count them all. Unfortunately, I had a harder time trying to find errors the court had made. It seemed to me that the court really didn't make too many errors in the case, but the defense attorney was another story. He made a ton.

And, at this point, I was cynical. I had seen what happened when people were corrupted by the system, and I knew there was a good chance the defense attorney might've been paid off to throw the case. Of course, I had no proof of that, but I did know that he was extraordinarily incompetent. I also knew that *somebody* would be convicted of raping this poor woman. An A-list actress was raped, beaten so badly that she was practically in a coma, she lost her memory, and she had to have extensive plastic surgeries to return her to normal. Somebody would pay for that. So, after reading through the facts of the case, and the transcripts, I realized that what happened was that somebody would pay for doing that to her, and Jamel was unfortunately the closest person the prosecutor could find to pin the blame on.

The reason why I was convinced the true culprit was somebody well-connected was just the fact that so many things had gone wrong in this case. It wasn't *just* that the defense attorney did not object to things that were clearly objectionable, and there were quite a few things that were objectionable, and it wasn't *just* the fact that the defense attorney failed to put on exculpatory evidence, such as showing the walls of the compound were way too tall for a small boy like Jamel to have scaled. It was everything about this case. It stunk to high heaven.

"Jamel, here's the thing," I said to him. "At this point, I don't think you really have a choice but to trust me. What do you have to lose? You just told me you don't have the money to hire somebody to file an appeal for you, so, as I see it, it's either me or nobody. You're already convicted of raping Felicity McDaniel. You have a chance to actually get out of your prison sentence, and that chance lies with one person – me."

He shook his head. "No, don't get me wrong. I know what you're saying, and I know that if somebody don't help me, I'm going to spend the rest of my life in prison for something I had nothing to do with. But I just don't know what's in it for you."

I took a deep breath. "Listen, here's the thing. I went to law school because I knew far too many of my friends who were going into the joint for nonviolent drug offenses. That's how they cleaned up my neighborhood – cops would sweep anybody and everybody who was caught with so much as a joint and make sure they got the book thrown at them. Of course, the only people who were subjected to this kind of treatment were minorities – the black and brown people. On the other hand, I could stand on the street corner and smoke a joint and cops would drive by me and look the other way. But if there was a black boy, or a Hispanic boy, or girl for that matter, they couldn't do anything on the street. If they had so much as a dime bag on their person, they were harassed, and, trust me, the cops harassed people on my street and they would be charged with intent to distribute and be put away for a long time. So after seeing one person after another on my street go to prison for what should have been a misdemeanor possession, I decided to do something about it. The thing that I decided to do was to go to law school so that I could help people like the people I grew up with."

At this, Jamel smiled. "Come on, you're putting me on. You're not from the streets."

"Why do you say that?"

"Look at you. You got lots of money, I can tell." He was looking at my Rolex watch and he nodded approvingly. "That watch costs more than what my mama makes in an entire year. Twice as much as what she makes. I can just tell it's not hot. I mean, you get these clowns in the hood selling that shit on the street, but you know it's made in Taiwan and it's going to break by the end of the day. But I can tell that that's the real shit right there. No, you ain't never been on the streets. But that's all right. I'm sure you have your reasoning for trying to get me out of this place. I think you probably just want the publicity, but, as my mama says, I'm not going to look no gift horse in the mouth."

I was telling him the truth about my neighborhood. It was a rough place to grow up, especially if you're a minority. But I knew I presented as a rich guy and I wasn't going to convince this kid otherwise, so I let it go.

"That's good. Listen, here's what I'm going to do. I'm going to take your case and file a notice of appeal immediately. I think we have a very good chance of getting your conviction overturned, but in the meantime, I really want to prove your actual innocence. I know there was no DNA found on Felicity, so it's going to be difficult to try to prove your innocence, but I'm going to try to do just that. At any rate, even if I can't show the appellate court that you're actually innocent, I want to make the case for your new trial. And I can almost assure you that you'll get a new trial."

I took a deep breath, hoping I wasn't promising too much. It wasn't like me to make a claim like I just made to him – that I could for sure get him off his charge. But, at the same time, I knew there was a good chance that would happen.

Jamel was looking at me now, his eyes scrunched up and with a look on his face like he just could not understand anything about what was going on. "Listen, I'm okay with walking this prison sentence down. I got a brother in the system, half-brother really, and he tells me things aren't so bad behind bars. To tell the truth, I was having a hard time trying to make ends meet on the streets. I mean, I was driving Uber and all that shit, but they don't pay nothing.

And you know that most of the money that I was making through Uber was going into the tank. I ain't got a pot to piss in and that's the truth. Listen, I know kids like me, we don't get a lot of breaks in this world. We certainly don't get to have defense attorneys just take our cases for free. I still don't know what your game is, but you're right about one thing – you are the only game in town for me. So, I'll let you represent me."

I took a deep breath. My home base was in San Diego, of course, and this kid was convicted in Los Angeles County. But he was being taken to the Victorville prison, and that would've been the same thing if he would have been convicted in San Diego County, so I figured that it wouldn't be too much of a burden to represent him.

I left him with a handshake and an assurance that I would be working on his case as soon as possible.

I called Avery in my car on the way home.

"I saw Jamel and he's going to be my new client."

"Are you sure about this?" Avery was concerned about my taking on this case because she knew it would be hard on me if I lost. She also knew that it would be hard on me to travel, because the District Court of Appeals was here in Los Angeles County. But, at the same time, I knew I didn't have to really make too many appearances in court, so it really wasn't that big of a deal for me.

What would be somewhat hard on me was the fact that I was determined to find the real person who had raped this woman, which meant I would have to make a lot of trips up to Los Angeles to try to figure that one out. I would have to talk to a lot of people, and I would have to make more than one pilgrimage to the actual site where she was raped. But, for the time being, it was just a matter of me getting back to my office in San Diego and combing through the transcripts

Insanity Defense

for all the errors, and then doing my research, writing out a brief, and scheduling an oral argument as soon as possible.

"I'm serious as a heart attack about this. Listen, this kid has no money and if I don't represent him, he's going to have to represent himself. Or find a jailhouse lawyer and we know how good they are." Truth be told, I knew quite a few people who were good jailhouse lawyers, but at the same time, they weren't exactly lawyers. They were just inmates who knew their way around the prison research libraries, and other inmates hired them to try to write out their appeals. That's how most inmates actually did their appeals, because there is not a right to an appellate counsel under the Constitution, so, once you're convicted, and you're poor, it's very difficult to find somebody to take your case, because you're not eligible for the public defender's office anymore.

"Okay, just remember you have a full roster of other cases right here in San Diego County, so you can't put too much time into this case. But if you feel strongly this kid is innocent and he didn't get a break, then, by all means, go for it."

I knew Avery would be all for my taking this case because of her background of being wrongfully convicted herself. It turned out that, in her case, the person who actually murdered her friend was a rich bastard by the name of Carl. He was running a sex trafficking ring, one that was well attended by very well-heeled people, and he had plenty of protection.

Why did I think it would be a similar case here?

Wrongful Conviction: Chapter Two

JAMEL

JAMEL WENT BACK to his cell after he saw the white guy who would try to actually see if he could get him out of prison. He knew he was about to be transferred to Victorville, and, as far as he knew, white guy or no, he would spend the rest of his life behind bars. That was just something he had come to terms with long ago.

Oh, he was grateful somebody had taken an interest in him. He just didn't think anything would come of it. He knew the score. He was a black kid, disposable. In fact, he wasn't just disposable, but a lot of people actively hated him just for the color of his skin. He knew that, within the past few years, the racism that had always been bubbling beneath the surface of this country had started boiling over. Suddenly, he was being attacked with racial slurs, almost daily, and people were always calling the cops on him for the slightest things. Such as the time he was in the park just laying in the grass. He had a blanket underneath him and was just enjoying the day. Some guy called the cops on him, apparently telling the cops that he was a homeless guy in the park and had to be dealt with. The cops came out and questioned him. He had to show the cops that he did actually have a home. In fact, the cops escorted him there. If he didn't have a home, he thought he probably would've spent the night in jail as a vagrant.

Another time, he was going into his apartment but had forgotten his key-card. This was when he actually had a full-time job, working construction, so he could afford a place of his own. He had since lost that job, due to budget cut-backs, and had been driving Uber ever since. On the day he forgot his key-card, he waited until somebody else entered the building and then went in with him. As he walked into the building, a white lady questioned him. She said she hadn't seen him around before, and she saw he didn't have a key card, so what was he doing there? He tried to show her that he had a key to his own apartment, but that didn't satisfy her. She also called the cops, who came out to question him, and, once again, he had to prove to the cops that he had an apartment in that building.

He knew that if he didn't have black skin that there was no way anyone would ever call the cops on him for simply relaxing in the park or getting into his own building, but he also knew that lots of his friends were also having the cops called on them for no real reason. Living while black was a crime anymore, and he knew that had gotten worse over the years and was just going to get worse and worse.

So, when he was arrested for raping this woman, even though he was the one who called 911, and if it weren't for him, she probably would've died, he knew he would get convicted for it. It was a foregone conclusion in his mind. This lady was raped, there was nobody else who would have the crime pinned on them, he was in the wrong place at the wrong time, and none of that mattered. What mattered was that he couldn't afford to hire an attorney, so he was assigned one, and the attorney he was assigned could not have cared less about his case. In fact, Jamel had the distinct impression that his attorney just wanted to get it over with, mainly because the case had attracted so much publicity, and his attorney, Jim Stack, didn't like the glare. Which was a reason why, when it came time to ask him to put on evidence on his behalf, Jim told the court he would rest. That meant he didn't call any witnesses and did not put on any kind of evidence on his behalf.

What was so sad was that Jamel just kind of shrugged his shoulders about his attorney's laziness and incompetence. He figured that was what he deserved, in a society like this that was not colorblind in any way, shape or form. He figured that it was just another way for a kid like him to get off the streets, not that he was ever on the streets, because, after all, he did have a job. Yes, it was a job driving Uber, so it didn't pay a whole lot. He was now living in a rented room that he found for only $500 a month, a tiny room in an old dilapidated house on the east side of Los Angeles, but, nevertheless, it was a home. His home. So, even though he knew the jury looked at him like he was a street kid, he really wasn't. He didn't deal drugs. He didn't gang bang. His mama had taught him right from wrong and kept him away from all that.

Yet, there he was, in jail awaiting transfer to the big house.

The tragedy was that he didn't even think it was necessarily unfair. It was what it was.

So even though this white boy, this Christian Davis boy, wanted to work his case, he didn't think it would come to anything. He just figured Christian would try to get him a new trial, but there was nothing that could be done for a guy like him.

Still, he was happy that Christian was even going to try.

Grab your copy...
vinci-books.com/wrongful-conviction

About the Author

Rachel Sinclair was a criminal defense attorney for eleven years, so she doesn't scare easily. She graduated from the University of Missouri-Kansas City School of Law in 1998, and worked for the Public Defender's Office for several years before striking out on her own. She currently lives in San Diego, California, with her boyfriend, Joey, and her two fur babies, Annie and Toby. In her spare time, she likes to read, bicycle all over town, Boogie Board at the beach, and watch trashy television.